"The person behind this doesn't have respect for law enforcement. They think they're above the law. They've killed once, and they won't hesitate to do it again. If we get close, our lives might be in danger."

Blake shook her head. "Just because we made a mistake in there," she said, pointing to the office, "doesn't mean that you have to be dramatic. We're fine."

Her words made goose bumps rise on his arms. Any time he'd ever gotten complacent in his job, or thought he was safe, was when he'd found himself in trouble.

"Think about it, Blake." Her name felt like velvet on his tongue; it even tasted sweet. He paused as he just looked at her for a moment.

"What?" she asked, locking eyes with him. And when she did, all he could think about was closing the distance between them.

Dust Up with the Detective

DANICA WINTERS

MILLS & BOON

First Published in Great Britain 2016
By Mills & Boon, an imprint of HarperCollins*Publishers*
1 London Bridge Street, London, SE1 9GF

Large Print edition 2016

© 2016 Danica Winters

ISBN: 978-0-263-06668-5

Our policy is to use papers that are natural, renewable and recyclable products and made from wood grown in sustainable forests. The logging and manufacturing processes conform to the legal environmental regulations of the country of origin.

Printed and bound in Great Britain
by CPI Antony Rowe, Chippenham, Wiltshire

Danica Winters is a multiple award-winning, bestselling author who writes books that grip readers with their ability to drive emotion through suspense and occasionally a touch of magic. When she's not working, she can be found in the wilds of Montana, testing her patience while she tries to hone her skills at various crafts—quilting, pottery and painting are not her areas of expertise. She believes the cup is neither half-full nor half-empty, but it better be filled with wine. Visit her website at danicawinters.net.

To Herb—
You make everything possible.
Always and forever.

Acknowledgments

This book wouldn't have been possible without the help of my community. Major thanks to the Missoula County Sheriff's Office and Brenda Bassett for their time and patience in helping to answer questions. Sergeant Prather, it was an honor to have had the opportunity for a ride along and to pick your brain. Your advice was invaluable. And to all those who serve our communities, you and your family's sacrifice are appreciated. You help to make the world a better place.

Chapter One

Everything in Montana was measured by time, not miles driven, not quality and not sacrifice. For example, the trip from Missoula to Butte took just under two hours. And her boyfriend? Nearly three months. At sixteen, the relationship had been too short to be called serious, yet long enough to leave her with a child. Then, in less than ten seconds, the relationship was over and she had been left with a beautiful daughter and fading dreams.

That was thirteen years ago. Thirteen terrifying, humbling and gratifying years. Nights spent soothing her daughter when she had ear infections, and days spent struggling to get where she was—a sheriff's officer with a steady job and a stable income. She was the only one strong enough to support her mother and her daughter. They needed her.

Dreams were for those who could afford them—and that would never be Blake West.

Her antiquated patrol unit's radio crackled to life as the 9-1-1 dispatcher's voice filled the car. "Blake, your mom called. Said there's some kind of issue up at your place."

She picked up the handset. "Dispatch, feel free to remind my mother that nine-one-one is to be used for emergencies only."

"You tell your mother that," the woman said with a laugh.

Blake shook her head, as she thought about telling her throwback-to-another-era Irish mother that she wasn't to do something. Blake had a better chance of convincing the Pope to give up being Catholic.

"Really, though," the dispatcher continued, "she said your cell wasn't working. She sounded really upset."

Blake picked up her cell phone. Just like half of Silver Bow County, there was no service today where yesterday there had been—just another perk of living in a state where technology was an unreliable amenity.

"Is Megan okay?"

"She didn't say. Just said she needed you to come home."

Blake stepped on the gas as she turned the car down the set of roads that led to their house. "If she calls back, tell her I'm on my way."

She flicked on her lights and sped down the pothole-ravaged road that led to the house on the outskirts of the mining-centered city of Butte. At one time the historical city had been beautiful with its brick buildings and Old West charm. There had been an uptick in the mine's activities around the city in the 1990s, but now it was a decaying mass of run-down miner's row houses and the home of a pit full of water so toxic that it even killed the birds that dared to land on its surface.

Most of those left in town were small-time miners, those who hoped the large mine operations would open again someday, or those who had retired from the Pit. It was the city of the strong, a city of survivors—just like Blake and her mother.

Gemma West could handle anything. If she was as upset as the dispatcher said, something had to be majorly wrong.

Had something happened to Megan? She was

old enough to know the rules, but that didn't mean she hadn't done something to put herself in danger.

Blake took a series of long breaths as she forced herself to remain calm.

Megan was probably fine.

She pulled to a stop in front of their beige ranch-style home, which rested behind a mature, though chemically stunted, pine. Near its base was a scar from her father's car the day he'd left so many years ago. She'd always hated and loved that tree. It was a visible reminder of days and lives spent scratching and tearing away in the mines that were the fulcrum of the corrupt city and how that city and its vices had destroyed her family. No matter how many years went by, the tree would never grow, never change. Too much damage had been done.

"Mom! Megan?" she yelled, hoping they would step out the front door to meet her.

It was dead quiet. She made her way up the steps and opened the aluminum screen door with a rattle.

"Mom, you home? Megan?" she called, her voice nearing frantic tones only a dog could hear.

The smell of home cooking, the kind done by generations who didn't care about waistlines or cholesterol, wafted from the kitchen.

"Mom?" she asked, moving toward the scent of fried chicken.

Something was terribly wrong. Her mother could hear a car coming from ten miles down the road, and she was notorious for meeting Blake at the front door, judgment in hand.

She moved to call for her daughter but

stopped as the sound of the back door's rusty hinges screeched.

She wasn't alone.

Out of instinct, she reached down and put her hand on her Glock, unclicking the snap that held it safely in its holster. After slipping the gun out, she raised it, ready to meet whatever or whomever she would find in the kitchen.

The old wooden floor creaked as she tried to sneak down the hall. Pressing her back against the wall, she readied herself.

Had someone broken in? Was someone trying to take her daughter?

Her daughter.

She lowered her gun. Maybe it was just Megan. The girl loved to surprise her—to jump out from behind walls and make her scream. If it was, she couldn't let her law enforcement training come into play. She couldn't risk hurting someone she loved.

"Megan, is that you?" she asked, trying to sound playful instead of terrified. "Pumpkin, you need to answer me." She lowered her gun and hid it behind her hip as she eased around the corner and into the kitchen.

On the counter under the window, a fresh plate of fried chicken sat cooling, its oil oozing into the paper towel underneath. A can of beans was next to the plate, the can opener still resting on its lip, as if her mother had been opening it but had suddenly been called away.

A movement outside caught her eye as something scuttled across the backyard and disappeared behind the shed.

The hair on her arms rose. *What is going on?* She took a step toward the back door.

Megan's scream pierced the air. The sound resonated from the darkened shed.

Blake ran outside. Gun raised. Ready. If someone was hurting her daughter, they would die.

Through the thin particleboard door of the shed, she heard muffled voices. She stopped, trying to quiet her breathing as she listened. She could barely make out her mother's voice.

She moved to the door. "Get down! Get down on the ground!" she yelled, kicking open the door, smashing it against the wall.

Megan was sitting at the table, her back to her. A man stood in the shadows, his arm raised. He was holding something.

"Put down your weapon!" Blake ordered.

The man moved, and a thin light from the tiny, dirt-covered window reflected off the blade of a hacksaw.

"I said put down your weapon!" She aimed her gun at his center mass.

The man looked at her. In the shadows she could make out only the whites of his eyes and the slight movement of his lips as he started to speak.

"Mom, no!" Megan turned around. Her round face was covered in sweat, and her eyes were wide with fear.

She raised her hands. Her wrists were in shackles.

Blake's finger trembled on the trigger as the man slowly lowered his weapon to the floor. "What in the hell do you think you are doing to my daughter?"

Chapter Two

"Not every situation requires a gun," Gemma said as she walked up the steps to the back door. "You scared poor Megan. Didn't she, honey?" Her mother wrapped her arm around her daughter and gave her a reassuring squeeze.

"I'm fine, Grandma, really." Megan tried to wiggle out of her embrace.

Blake snorted lightly. If the girl was a bit older, she would have realized that, for good or bad, no matter how much she struggled, she would never be out of Gemma West's grip.

"I'm sorry about this mess, Jeremy. Having

a gun pointed at you isn't much of a thank-you for your help in trying to get Megan out of those handcuffs," her mother continued.

Blake looked over at Jeremy Lawrence. She'd always thought of him as the gangly neighbor she had once had a crush on, but seeing the grown-up detective now, it was clear he was nothing like the boy she remembered. Now he stood tall with impossibly wide shoulders, a chiseled jaw and the piercing green eyes of a stranger. Everything from the way he walked, solid and firm, to the way he watched their every move, in control and ever vigilant, screamed alpha man.

"You're a tough one, Megan," Jeremy said as he held the door for them. "You remind me of my daughter. I think you'd like her. Once she got ahold of my handset and started play-ing Simon Says on the radio. It was funny, except for the fact that it was on a live channel. I thought the dispatchers were going to lose it." He turned to Blake and smiled like he understood what she was going through as a single mother.

She gave him a thankful nod, but he couldn't possibly know how hard it was. How each day she was plagued with Mom-guilt—the overwhelming fear that no matter what choices she made, she should be doing more for her daughter. As it was, she tried her best to be there for Megan, but because of the crazy nature of her job and her unconventional schedule, Megan was often left with her grandmother—who never missed an opportunity to remind Blake of all the things she could do better.

There was no way Jeremy could understand all the hats she had to wear to make it through the day.

"Were you mad when your daughter messed up, Mr. Lawrence?" Megan asked him as she made her way into the house.

Jeremy shook his head as he smiled at Blake. "It was my fault. It hadn't occurred to me she would play with my scanner."

"See, Mom, he wasn't mad when his daughter screwed up." Megan looked back at her as if gauging her residual anger.

"I'm not mad," Blake said as she followed her mother and daughter inside. "I just don't understand what possessed you to take my handcuffs out of my drawer and put them on. You had no business—"

Jeremy put his hand on her lower back as he followed her inside and let the door close behind them. His hot, familiar touch made her stop midsentence.

"I'm sure she didn't mean to upset you,

Blake. Did you, Meg?" he asked, smiling as he gently moved his hand away, leaving behind the warmth of his touch.

Did he know what he was doing to her? The last man who had touched her, at least in that way, had been Megan's father. Sure, she and Jeremy had known each other as children, but he couldn't touch her so familiarly—not when their friendship had existed a lifetime ago.

"I'm sorry, Mom," Megan said.

"Jeremy's right. It's your mom's fault," Gemma said as she moved through the kitchen. "If she wouldn't have left the handcuffs where you could find them, none of this would have happened." She turned to face Blake. "And it would have been nice if you would have answered your phone."

She loved her mom, but the jab pierced deep, puncturing the little bubble of guilt that she tried to keep out of reach. Her mother was right; she had messed up. She shouldn't have left her cuffs where Megan could find them. But… "Mother, I have no control over where and when my phone works—you know this."

"Well, I don't think you have any business traipsing around the county without a phone that works. Do I need to call the sheriff to make sure you get a satellite phone?"

She looked to Jeremy. He didn't need to hear any of this. The last thing she needed was another officer thinking she was incompetent, or worse—that she needed her mother to fight her battles.

He gave her a Cheshire-cat grin, the same mischievous grin that he'd always used to get them out of trouble when they were kids.

"Mrs. West, is that your famous fried

chicken?" He motioned toward the plate on the counter.

Her mother took the bait, brightening up at the chance to feed a man. "Oh, are you hungry? Why don't you have a bite?" True to her nature, the question was more an order than a request. "I'll throw the beans on, and it'll be ready in a jiff."

"That sounds great, but I need to get running home. I'm just up from Missoula for the night."

"Really? Is everything okay?" From the look on her face, it seemed like Gemma meant the question to come from a place of concern, but her voice made it clear that she was more curious than empathetic. As if she looked forward to some thread of gossip that she could share at the next bunco party.

"I'm sure everything's okay. Right, Jeremy?" Blake hinted, hoping that he would take this as his chance to get out before he and his family became the central focus of the Butte Red Hatters Bunco Club for the next six months.

He looked at her, his eyes shimmering with something she could have sworn resembled lust, but she shrugged it off. There was no way he would be interested in her. He was married.

She glanced down at his ring finger—his ring was missing. *That's right...* He'd gotten a divorce. When her mother had told her about it a few months past, she had pushed the news aside as irrelevant. Yet, with him standing in front of her, it seemed more relevant than ever. The knot in her gut tightened as she forced herself to look away from his naked hand.

Even if he wasn't married, he wouldn't want her. No man would want to take on a single mom who lived with her mother and was struggling to make it in a small-town sheriff's department—unless he was a glutton for punishment.

"Things are a little rough. You know…family drama."

Her mother perked up. "What's going on?"

"It's just my brother. He's going through a hard time."

"Is that right," her mother chimed. "Is there anything I can do?"

"Thanks, Mrs. W, but it'll be all right." Jeremy sent her a grateful but guarded smile. "Unfortunately, I'll have to pass on the chicken—but it smells great," he added, as her mother's face fell.

"Oh, okay," she said, her voice specked with disappointment, the kind that always moved Blake into doing whatever it was Gemma truly wanted.

Jeremy's body tensed, his biceps pressing

hard against his cotton T-shirt. Apparently, Gemma West's shaming worked on someone besides her. Why did her mother have to put everyone under her spell?

Megan thumped down in the chair by the dining table. "Mom, I'm hungry."

"Thank you, Jeremy, for helping us out," Blake said, motioning toward her daughter.

He glanced at her and smiled again. The way he looked at her made her temperature rise. No one had looked at her like that, like she really existed as something more than a mother or a sheriff's deputy, in a long time.

She turned away as she scolded herself. He was just looking at her. It didn't mean anything. She was lonely. She needed to get a handle on her emotions. Crushes were for those who had a chance—which she didn't.

He needed to go. She simply could not be around a man like him.

"I need to get back to work. After you?" She walked to the door and opened it, motioning for him to leave.

He turned to walk out.

"I hope everything goes well with your brother. By the way, which brother is it?" her mother called behind him, throwing a speed bump into Blake's plans.

Jeremy looked back over his shoulder. "Robert."

"Where's Casper these days?" her mother continued.

Blake's sweaty hand slipped on the open door.

"He's working up north with Border Patrol."

"That's wonderful," her mom said, turning to her with a raise of the eyebrow. She flashed a glance back at Jeremy, like she was trying to coach Blake on how to get him to stay. "Isn't that nice, Blake?"

"Yes, that's great, Mother."

Jeremy chuckled. "If you need me again, Mrs. W, I'll be in town for a couple of days." He brushed against Blake as he made his way out the door. His touch magnified the need she was trying her best to ignore. "Hey, if you need a break, maybe we could meet up sometime," he whispered so low that only she could hear.

In a flash, she was back in high school, and they were planning to sneak out of the house. The thrill of being caught and the excitement that came with breaking the rules filled her. Just as quickly as the feelings rose, she stomped them out. She wasn't sixteen. She was a mother. And her daughter came first—no matter how badly she wanted to take Jeremy up on his offer.

"Thanks, but maybe next time you're in town."

He nodded, but there was a faint look of hurt deep in his eyes as he turned away. She couldn't help taking one last look as he walked away. His jeans were the kind with the fancy stitching on the back pockets, the kind that always drew a person's eye to them and, in this case, to his perfectly round behind.

Clearly the man worked out.

Dang it.

She forced herself to look away. What was wrong with her today?

She could feel her mother's eyes boring into her back. She needed to leave, to get to work, but she let the door close as she turned back to her family.

"That right there is why you don't have a man in your life," her mother said with a *tsk* as she flurried around the kitchen, getting the potato salad out of the fridge.

"Maybe I don't have a man in my life because I don't want one," Blake retorted. Instantly she wished she hadn't, because it would only allow her mother to continue on her soapbox.

"That Jeremy, he's got a good head on his shoulders. You need a man like him. You would get one, if you weren't so hard to please."

That was the pot calling the kettle black.

"Here you go, sweetie." Her mother set a plate of fried chicken and potato salad in front of Megan and went back to the can of beans.

"Thanks, Grandma."

Blake glanced down at her watch. "I need to go." She gave Megan a kiss on the top of the head while her daughter chomped away. "Please don't get into any more of my things."

"Wait," her mother said. "Why don't you eat first?"

There was a rumble in her stomach, but she had to escape the mess that was her personal life. Work was so much easier. "I'm good, Mom."

"Fine then." Her mother's disdain was palpable. "At least take the rest of this food over to Jeremy and his family as a thank-you. You know, he didn't have to come over here to help us. It was just lucky he was even around. We could have been all day if we had to wait for you."

The sharp edge of her mother's words deepened her wounds. It wasn't that she didn't want to be closer to her family, but she had to work. She had to support the people she loved most, even if they sometimes forgot how much pressure she was under.

Her mother covered the plate of chicken with plastic wrap, then shoved it into Blake's hands. "Now run along. And don't get lost with my chicken." Her mother pushed her out the door. "And make sure you let his mother know that I'd like my plate back."

It was like she was eight years old again, her mother moving her along in her pursuit toward her own means. She would never be exactly what Gemma wanted her to be, would always be a disappointment, constantly seeking her mother's approval and trying to make her proud. No matter how badly she wanted them to, some things would never change.

Chapter Three

Splitting the blanket. Trimming away the dead-weight. Losing one's other half. Detective Jeremy Lawrence had heard them all, but they all meant one thing: he was divorced.

He thumbed the empty place on his ring finger where his wedding band used to be.

Genevieve had made such a big deal about the ring when they were first together. She hadn't wanted him to wear yellow gold, claiming it would clash with her engagement ring—a ring she'd also picked out—and he couldn't get silver as it would tarnish. He'd felt like an idiot standing there in the jewelry store getting told that tungsten was really the best option for him, but at twenty-two he'd been young and dumb and willing to put up with anything if it meant he got to marry her. Heck, he'd thought himself lucky. She'd been the cheerleader, the girl who could light up a room with a smile and, better yet, make him burn with want with the mere trailing of her fingertips.

Everything, all the way down to her name, had to be classy.

The marriage had been over the minute she had figured out he was just a regular guy, not the idealized version she must have had in her mind.

He reached in his pocket, pulled out the ring and let it drop on his dresser, the dresser he'd had since he was a child. It was funny how a piece of unloved furniture could last longer than a marriage. If nothing else, it proved that a dead oak was stronger than a life built on feelings. Maybe there really was something to being cold, lifeless…at least you could weather the storms.

None of it mattered. He'd gotten a daughter out of their screwed-up marriage. He could be thankful for that, even if Penny didn't live with him. At least he had something to hold on to.

His father's footsteps echoed down the hall toward his room; there was a knock on the door. "Jeremy, you in there?"

"Yeah, Dad. What do you need?"

"Your mother's wondering when you're going to run out to Robert's. It would be good if you could get out there before dark," his father said, as if he hadn't heard them fighting over Robert for the last ten minutes.

It was funny; he'd been home just a few

hours, but when he had set foot in the door it was like he had stepped back in time—parents fighting, brother missing and him searching for a way to escape. Just like when he'd been a kid, he'd found refuge at the neighbors', but instead of being the one who needed to be saved, this time he'd paid them back for all the times Mrs. W was there for him. Finally things were coming full circle.

And just like the past, Blake had rushed him to the door while she made a point of being out-of-bounds.

He took one last look at the ring, now at home tucked safely away in his past. "I was just about to head out," he told his father.

"Good," his father said, turning to leave. "Oh, and Blake is here. Brought over some supper as a thank-you."

He figured Mrs. W must have forced her to

come over. It really was like all those years ago. He loved his family, but he needed to get the hell out of Butte and away from the ghosts that haunted this place—regardless of how beautiful one particular ghost was.

Blake stood in the living room, her hand on the doorknob. She was talking to his mother, who was sitting in her recliner. Blake's uniform top was stretched tight over her bulletproof vest. The buttons gaped slightly, revealing a T-shirt underneath. As she moved, he caught a quick glimpse of her black bra strap, and he felt his body shift in response. There was just something so *right* about a woman who wore a uniform and sexy lingerie underneath.

He wanted to rip open her shirt and her vest, kiss the lines of her lacy bra, slip what he figured would be matching black panties down her legs.

Jeremy forced himself to look away, focusing on the painting of a meadow that had hung on the living room wall so long that there was a faint brown smoke line around it.

"Blake was just telling me that she has seen Robert lately," his mother started. "Isn't that right, Blake?"

Blake nodded.

"Apparently she was out to his place a few weeks ago." His mother tapped her fingers on the armrests of her chair.

"It wasn't anything that major," Blake offered. "There was just a minor dispute. It was in the *Montana Standard*. I thought you must have heard."

He hadn't read the local newspaper in years, but Blake was right. It was surprising his mother hadn't gotten a call from the phone tree. Her friends lived for nothing more than to read the obituaries and scan through the weekly police blotter.

"What happened?" Jeremy asked.

Blake chewed on her lower lip, and her gaze flickered to his mother, as if there was something that she didn't want to say in front of her. "You know, just the normal thing."

"Was it something to do with his wife?" His mother turned to him. "Tiffany has been threatening to leave him for months now. I told you that Robert needed your help. I wish you could've been here earlier, Jeremy."

"Well, Mom, you know how it is. Work's been busy," he said, but he was focused on Blake and how she shifted her weight from one foot to the other.

His mother said something under her breath that he was only too glad he couldn't hear.

He made his way to Blake and opened the door. "You busy this afternoon?"

Blake glanced down at her watch. "Why?"

He waited for her to step outside and let the door close behind him. "I'd appreciate it if you can fill me in on what's going on with my brother," he told Blake.

She waved goodbye to his mother through the glass storm door. "Look, I appreciate what you did with Megan, but I don't want to get involved with you or whatever it is you have going on."

"Whoa." He breathed out, unsure why she had been so abrupt. "I just thought—"

She raised her hand. "No, stop. I shouldn't have lost my temper. I'm not upset with you. It's just my mother." She motioned toward her house.

She had every right to be upset after what

she had walked into. It would have taken more than a little fried chicken to talk him down if he'd walked into a scene with someone holding a hacksaw over his daughter's head. Unlike her, he didn't know if he could have held back from shooting.

His gaze drifted to the utility belt at her waist. "Lots of calls coming in?" he asked as they walked across the lawn toward her house.

She slipped out her cell phone and glanced down at it. "To be honest, no. But I should be on patrol."

"What time do you get off?"

"Not for a few more hours."

"Well, if you aren't busy, I would really appreciate you running to Robert's with me."

She looked up at him, her blue eyes reflecting the color of the sky.

"I would hate to be walking into a mess up

there." He silently hoped she would say yes, and it wasn't just because he wanted her to tell him about Robert. It had to do with the desire that seemed to rise in him every time he caught a glimpse of her.

"You heading up there now?" she asked him.

He nodded.

She nibbled her lip again, making him wonder if he made her as uncomfortable as she made him. "I did want to talk to Robert, make sure everything had smoothed out. You could ride with me, but you know—"

"I'll follow you up there." He motioned toward his truck. "I'd hate to get you in trouble. We have to follow protocol."

There was a hint of a smile as she looked at him. "You say that, but we both know you've always been the kind who likes to make his own rules."

ROBERT'S HOUSE SAT off a dirt road, shrouded by trees and brush. On the neighboring property, old cars and trailers in varying stages of rust were parked in a haphazard pattern. Between the rusting carcasses were piles of downed trees and garbage. A few of the detritus hills were covered with tarps whose prime of life had passed years ago and now were nothing more than weathered strings broken up by little squares of blue.

He'd always hated this place, the world his brother called home. The drive that led to Robert's house was a steady climb, and Blake was taking it at a crawl in her patrol unit, twisting and turning as she attempted to miss the washed-out ruts in the dirt. This wasn't the kind of place in which one wanted to find oneself stranded. Everything about the deep woods spoke of danger, from the road all the way down to the twisted faces that peered out from the windows of the derelict homes they passed.

Rising from the brush was a building, still covered in Tyvek plastic wrap, as if any day the construction company would come back and finish siding the house they had built— only it had been years since they'd been there. The roof sagged in the middle from too many heavy snows and too little care.

His brother had always cared more about what was in the earth than what was on top of it, and it had even been that way with his wife, Tiffany. The poor woman had more than her fair share to deal with when it came to Robert. Then again, Jeremy wasn't in a spot to judge anyone else's relationship. For years, everyone had told him how great his marriage was, yet behind closed doors it was a different story—

late-night fights about his schedule, the stress that came with being in law enforcement and the money. In the end, there was never enough money, time or even love.

Blake pulled to a stop and got out, waiting for him.

He parked next to her and met her at her car. "So, fill me in. What kind of trouble has my brother been getting himself into now?"

Robert had always fallen in and out of the bottle and usually directly into the hands of the law, leaving Jeremy to clean up his mess. The last time he'd talked to Robert they'd had one hell of a beer-fueled fight, ending with Robert on the ground and him promising to never lift another finger to save his brother's lousy carcass. Yet here he was again.

"I was called here a few weeks ago, but it wasn't for Tiffany, as your mother assumed."

Blake leaned against her patrol car, the round curve of her hips on full display. "This time, Robert was having an altercation with his neighbor, Todd O'Brien." She pointed in the direction of the property that was full of rusted-out shells of cars.

"This happen before?"

She nodded and gave a slight shrug. "You know how it is—most people out here live with a militia-like mentality. It's all about the guns, the freedom of speech and action. Out here the law is more of a recommendation than a reality. When something needs to be handled, vigilante justice reigns."

It was funny. No matter where you were in Montana—whether in the city of Missoula or the hillsides on the outskirts of Silver Bow County—some of the same problems arose. Usually they centered on two things: guns and liquor. Sometimes he couldn't help feeling like he lived in the Wild West.

Jeremy looked up at his brother's house. The lights were off, and the doors were closed. Leaves littered the front porch. "You think Robert said something, and it set this O'Brien off?"

"We couldn't make much of the situation. Neither wanted to press charges, but we left them both with a warning that they needed to bring the conflict down and keep it under control." She sighed. "Without one of them wanting to press charges, there wasn't much we could do. Your brother was pretty upset about the guns, though, wanted us to at least write O'Brien a ticket for a noise disturbance, but we hadn't heard any of it."

Jeremy nodded. "My brother has a way of pissing people off and getting in trouble. You out here often?" Somehow it felt like a poorly timed come-on.

She nodded, with a faint smile like she had heard it, too, but was letting it go. "Your brother has some issues…but I always said you can't judge someone by their family."

He raised an eyebrow. "You think?"

"I'm nothing like my mother—at least I hope not." She laughed. "And from what your mother's told me, I assume you're nothing like your brother."

There was something in her voice that made it clear she didn't necessarily like Robert. But did that mean she liked *him*? He shook the thought from his head. He couldn't read anything into this.

She made her way up the front porch and knocked on the door.

There was no answer.

"You think he's still working in the mine?" Blake asked.

"Probably. We can run down there and take a look. It's not too far," he said, motioning her to follow him as he led the way down the well-worn path that headed to the Foreman Mine.

Though he tried not to, he kept glancing back, making sure she was okay. Each time he checked on her, she looked away as if she was purposefully avoiding his gaze. The air between them filled with the crunch of dead pine needles as they hiked.

"He mine copper?" she asked, as if she was as uncomfortable with the silence between them as he was.

"Yep, but he finds gold and other heavy metals, as well. Makes a decent living, but you couldn't get me to do what he does."

"Mining is hard work."

"That's not it," he said. "I couldn't handle

being underground all day, every day." Though, as he said it, it reminded him of his own job. There he was usually sitting behind his desk, exploring the dark corners of a crime, looking for any clue that would lead to the mother lode.

"You scared of the dark?" She looked at him with a teasing smirk. "It's good to know that even a tough guy like you has a weakness."

It wasn't the dark he was afraid of. No…it was the fear of the world collapsing in around him. He'd already had it happen once when his marriage ended. He wasn't about to open himself up to such a failure again.

He glanced over at her, catching her gaze. "We all have weaknesses."

She slipped slightly, catching herself with the help of the branch of a small pine.

He took her hand. Her sweaty fingers gripped his just long enough for her to get her feet under her, but she quickly let go to brush herself off.

"Ha!" she said, her cheeks turning a light shade of red. "I guess my weakness is walking."

Jeremy laughed, the sound out of place in the quiet, stunted forest. For a moment he considered holding her hand the rest of the way down to the mouth of the mine, but she didn't seem like the type who wanted help, and he couldn't just elbow his way into her life—she wasn't his wife. She wasn't anything but a former crush. In truth, he didn't know her anymore. All he really knew was that she had her daughter, her mother and a job that, when she spoke of it, made her entire body tense.

He motioned for her to take the lead, admittedly because he wanted to watch her butt but ostensibly so he could make sure she was safe as she steadily made her way down the hill. He wasn't disappointed as he watched her. She moved with a quiet grace, smooth and steady as she carefully picked her way between the granite boulders as they headed into the maw of the earth.

Blake took out her flashlight and clicked it on. "Is this it?" she asked, motioning toward the dark, cavelike entrance.

In truth, it had been years since he'd been to the mine. The last time he'd been there the opening had been easily identifiable. Yet as she flashed her light downward, all he could make out were mounds of pegmatite-rich, reddish dirt.

"It should be here. Right here." He frowned. Grabbing his phone, he clicked on the light and moved into the muddy hole. "There should be a way in here." He prodded around, but the ground that filled the entrance shaft was as solid and compact as cement.

"Are you sure this is the place?" Blake asked.

"I thought so."

There was something wrong. The dirt in

the entrance was wet, but it hadn't rained in a month. And even though the dirt that filled the shaft's entrance was compact, the ground under their feet was loose, compressing as he shifted his weight. It had to have been freshly exposed.

He took a step forward. His toe caught on a loose rock, tripping him. He shone his light at the ground. Beneath the cobble that littered the area was a crushed lantern—the lantern Robert hung on the entrance of the mine any time he was underground.

"You don't think—" Blake started.

Jeremy stopped her with a raise of his hand. He couldn't stand hearing what he already knew—the mine had collapsed.

He prayed Robert wasn't inside, but the lamp told him all he needed to know. Robert was trapped, and there was only a slight chance he could still be alive.

Chapter Four

The insides of Jeremy's hands where covered in blisters. Dirt caked his nails, and his knuckles were bloody where he had torn them against the earth, but the job of freeing his brother had been too big for one man.

Blake watched the firefighters milling around outside the mine, taking a break from their attempts to break through the concrete-like blockade that filled its entrance. They had been at it for hours. They'd finally gotten an excavator on-site and received the go-ahead to start a full excavation. From the look on Jeremy's face, it had already taken too long.

Blake walked up the hill toward Robert's house and motioned for Jeremy to follow.

Jeremy walked beside her, his movement slow and numb. She had to do something, anything to help. For the second time that day, she felt powerless in her inability to control the events that swirled around them.

"Have you asked your parents if they've heard anything from Robert? Maybe he's tried to call?" As soon as the words left her lips, she knew they were in vain. Of course he couldn't call, but she had to say something to make the agonizing look on Jeremy's face disappear.

"There's no cell service in the mine—I can guarantee it." His eyes darkened, and his face tightened, the sexy lines around his eyes deepening. "Besides, there's no use in getting them up in arms. If we call them, they'll ask too many questions."

He was right. There was no sense alerting his parents that something was amiss if this was some kind of wild-goose chase. She could just imagine her mother getting a similar call. In a matter of minutes, Gemma West would have been on the scene and attempting to tell the crew exactly how they should be doing their jobs. No, family could wait.

She stepped up onto the porch and pressed her face against the window in the door. Inside Robert's one-room cabin was an open sofa bed and a wood-burning fireplace. The walls were covered in pictures of elk and bear, and a mounted trout hung over the kitchen window. A gun rack hung over the bed, and a small-caliber rifle sat nestled in its grips. It was as if the place had been intentionally stripped of all things feminine.

"Do you think it's possible Tiffany left him?" she asked.

Jeremy shrugged, staring ahead as if he was lost deep in thought.

"Is this what the house looked like the last time you were here?"

"What do you mean?" Jeremy moved beside her and peered inside.

"I…uh… I just mean I don't see anything of Tiffany's. Wouldn't you think if she was still living here you'd at least see a stray hair tie or something? It's almost like there hasn't been a woman here in a long time."

"Robert and Tiffany…" Jeremy gave a tired sigh. "They have more issues than *National Geographic*. They're constantly at each other's throats. If she left, good for her. It's the best for both of them."

Robert's personal life was in shambles. Could that have meant he would have wanted to end things? As a miner, he had everything he needed to cave in the mine's entrance. Maybe it had been his way of never being found.

On the table underneath the window was a ledger. She squinted through the glass as she tried to make out the penciled notes. She read the most recent one scrawled onto the time sheets.

September 23 Time in: 06:30 Time out:

The time out sat empty, echoing all the things it could possibly mean—or the one thing she feared most.

"Was your brother having any other issues?

Anything going on as far as his mental health is concerned?"

Jeremy stepped around to the bay window and peered in through the glass. "My mother said he's been agitated lately. Thought it had something to do with Tiffany."

"Any signs of depression?" She instinctively looked toward the sofa bed, where the sheets sat in a rumpled mess at the end of the mattress.

"I don't know. It's hard to say. Robert has always been one who kept his cards close to his chest."

There was something in Jeremy's voice, almost as if there were pangs of guilt that rested just under the surface of his words.

"Do you think he would have ever tried to commit suicide?"

Jeremy jerked.

She shouldn't have just thrown it out there. He was feeling something…some sort of guilt or perhaps vulnerability; she couldn't be sure. She should have been softer in her delivery, but the officer in her corrected her. She had to ask the questions that needed to be asked. She couldn't censor herself to spare his feelings.

"I would hope not," he finally answered. "I would hope he wouldn't do anything so stupid."

"Stupid?" She thought a lot of things about suicide, and what a mistake it was for anyone to take his or her own life, but rarely did she think it was stupid.

"That's not what I meant," Jeremy corrected himself. "I would just hope that he would ask for help before he made the choice to end things."

"You said he was tight-lipped."

"He is…but…" Jeremy's mouth puckered

and his eye turned storm. "Look, he's probably fine. Let's not go there, okay?"

He'd shut her down. Not that she could blame him. Maybe he was right. Maybe an accident had caused the cave-in, and Robert was sitting in the mine, hoping someone would find him.

"I'm sorry, Jeremy."

He seemed to force a smile, the lines of his lips curled in harsh juxtaposition to the rest of his face. "No...you're fine. If I was in your position, I'd be asking the same thing."

She nodded, not sure of what exactly to say that would make things less tense between them, but there was no fixing what riddled the air.

A fireman walked up the hill after them, stopping before he reached the porch. His cheeks were spattered with dirt and sweat.

"We've broken through. Looks like the mine shaft is intact."

"Great. That's great," Jeremy said. "Was there anything that could give us a clue as to why the mine entrance collapsed? Any evidence of explosives?"

The fireman shrugged, his sweaty shirt hugging his chest as he moved. "The excavator did the trick in getting us in, but it tore the hell out of everything. It's hard to say what you and your investigators will find."

Firefighters were like Wreck-It Ralph, always tearing and bulldozing away anything that stood in their way, but this was one of those times that Blake was happy to have their help.

They followed them down the hill, night trailing them. Ahead the fire crews had set up industrial-strength lights that burned away the darkness. All except for the oblong entrance of the mine, where the light disappeared like it was being sucked into a black hole.

"We haven't sent anyone in. We were waiting for you," the fireman said, stopping at the mouth of the cave.

"Robert!" Jeremy called, his voice echoing in the mine and cascading deep into the darkness.

There was no answer. Instead they were met with the excavator's treads rattling and clanging as a man drove it up the embankment and toward the waiting tractor trailer.

Jeremy moved forward, but Blake grabbed hold of his biceps, stopping him. "Wait."

"My brother's in there."

"I hear you, but we need to be careful."

Jeremy gazed into the mine.

Blake took out her notepad and turned to the firefighter who'd headed the excavation. "How deep was the cave-in?"

"It varied, but mostly everything was about ten to fifteen feet."

She made a note and, after sliding the camera from her pocket, took a picture of the scene. "But you didn't find evidence of an explosion?"

The fireman shook his head. "No, but look," he said, running his hand down a structural support beam they must have put into place to keep from having the mine fall back in on itself. "We found support beams like these every three feet. You'd have to check on the code, but with these four-by-fours like that, it seems like more than enough structural support to sustain the weight above. There's been no earthquakes, at least that I know of, and no major rainstorms or weather that would have caused the ground to give way. I'd bet my bottom dollar that someone did this on purpose. If it was imploded, it was with a low-grade explosive.

Nothing big enough to cause major damage, just enough firepower to get the job done."

Blake nodded, taking note of his opinion. It wouldn't be admissible in court, but at least she had an idea of what could have happened and she could write it up when she filed her report.

"Is it stable deeper in?" she asked.

The firefighter shrugged. "It's hard to say what you'll find. Oftentimes, explosions can have a bit of a cascading effect. If you go in, you need to make sure you take your time and be safe. You want me or one of my team to go in with you?"

"I've got it," Jeremy said. "I'll go in. There's no sense in you all going in and putting yourself in danger." He turned to look at her. "I don't want anyone to get hurt."

A faint heat rose in her cheeks, but she tried to staunch the fire. "Jeremy, you may be a detective, but this isn't your jurisdiction. You can't go in. It's my job."

"But this is my family."

If she were in his shoes, she wouldn't have taken no for an answer, either. She had to follow the rules, but it didn't feel right leaving him out. "Since you're the only person who's been in the mine, you can go in as a search volunteer. Nothing more. Don't touch anything. Got it?"

He nodded.

"Here," the fireman said, handing them each hard hats complete with headlamps. "You're going to need these."

They took them, and Jeremy put his on. In the night's shadows, he looked like a miner from an old tintype photograph, dirt smudging his cheeks and his eyelashes covered in dust.

"Let's go," Blake said, starting down the shaft.

The place smelled of dank, wet dirt and iron-rich minerals, the scent of deep earth—full and heady. The tunnel was wide enough for two to walk side by side with their shoulders rubbing against the walls. A tendril of claustrophobia wrapped around her, but she ignored the way it tightened around her chest and threatened to squeeze until panic oozed from every pore.

No. I'm strong. I can handle this.

She repeated the mantra over and over as she moved deeper, but it did little to quell her anxiety.

She walked, Jeremy close beside her, until the tunnel branched in a Y shape. She suddenly wished they had found a map, anything to help them avoid getting lost in the maze.

Jeremy took a large breath of air, like he was going to yell, but Blake shushed him. "Don't yell. If anything is unstable…" *We could be killed.* She resisted the urge to voice her fears. "Just don't."

He looked around them, like he could almost read her mind, and nodded.

A bead of earth slipped loose from the wall and cascaded down the side like an earthen waterfall.

"Right or left?" she asked, motioning toward the break in their path.

"Left. Robert never did anything right in his entire life." He gave a dry laugh.

She went left. The walls seemed to move in closer and the dark seemed even more ominous as they made their way deeper into the mountain. Each few hundred feet, the tunnel grew narrower, until she had to turn sideways to squeeze through. Her heart thrashed in her chest as her claustrophobia intensified.

She hated small spaces. What if she got stuck? What if the earth shifted around them and they were trapped? What would happen to Megan? What would happen to her mother?

The tunnel narrowed even more. Her chest brushed against the rock. And, as she exhaled, the warm air bounced off the rock in front of her and she could feel it on her cheek.

It was too close.

The walls were too close.

Jeremy was too close.

She couldn't do this.

Something ran over her shoe. She jumped with a squeal, slamming her hard hat into the top of the cave.

"I can't, Jeremy." She tried to control her breathing, but now it was coming in rapid, panicked heaves.

He took her hand, running his thumb over her skin. "Okay. It's okay," he soothed.

His heartbeat was so strong that she could

feel it through his grip. Did he hate this as much as she did?

Jeremy led her back down the tunnel from where they'd come, until he reached a spot wide enough for them both to stand. "Let me take the lead."

She nodded, but his voice sounded like it was coming through a can. The world spun around her slightly, forcing her to lean back against the wall and close her eyes. "Just a minute," she whispered.

"Are you okay?"

"I'm fine," she lied as her head started to throb and a faint wave of light-headedness washed over her. She pulled her hand from his, afraid that it wasn't just the claustrophobia or the bump to the head that was making her feel adrift.

She braced herself against the walls of the

cave. The earth was cool and damp under her touch, and the dirt had given way to hard rock. The jagged edges scraped her hands, but the pain made her come back to herself. Lifting her hand, she wiped a speckle of blood from her palm.

Jeremy took her face in his hands. "You're fine. Everything will be okay. You're safe with me."

In their little cocoon of warm yellow light, and wrapped in his hands, she believed him. She looked up into his face. She focused on the green depths of his eyes, blocking out every-thing else around her. After a while her breath-ing slowed as he caressed her face, moving a stray hair back from her neck.

"We won't have to be in here much longer," he whispered. "He has to be close."

Jeremy's warm fingertips brushed the skin

right under her bottom lip, his touch making the cold rock beneath her feel that much cooler. Leaning in, he stole her lips, kissing her with a tenderness far deeper than the mine.

Everything around her disappeared. There was only him. His mouth on hers. The luscious texture of his tongue as it brushed over the curve of her lip, lightly caressing hers. He flicked his tongue, making her thighs tense, warmth rise from her core and her thoughts rush to the other places his mouth could explore.

His hands roamed down her neck, over her curves and down her hips. He pulled her against him, pressing her against his responding body. She didn't know what it was. The fever with which he touched her, her long drought from masculine contact. Whatever it was, she kissed him back with a ravenous hunger. It felt—

From somewhere deep behind them, near the entrance of the cave, came the sound of a crackling radio. The high-pitch static cut through the air and brought Blake back to reality.

Jeremy jerked with the sound. "I… I… shouldn't have done that," he stammered, wiping his lips with the back of his hand. "I just meant to make you feel better. I'm sorry."

"You're right. You shouldn't have." She stepped away from him and out of the light in an attempt to cover the hurt that must have shown on her face. He wasn't the only one who had made a mistake. She shouldn't have let him kiss her. Now everything was going to get confusing.

"Let's go back. I think this way is blocked— it's getting too narrow." *Entirely* too narrow, as far as she was concerned. She couldn't be this close to him.

He started to say something but stopped. "Okay."

She led the way back, and, as they neared the Y, a warm breeze blew in from the entrance, making her aware of how cold it was in the cave. Between their moving and the kiss, she hadn't noticed the icy chill. If Robert was hurt somewhere in there, was it possible that he could have become hypothermic? If he couldn't move, in the damp cold of the mountain's underbelly it wouldn't have taken long.

She walked a little faster down the right branch of the tunnel, moving ahead of Jeremy just enough that she was outside the range of his light. Her foot struck something, and it sent her tumbling. Her shoulder connected with the floor, mud kicking up into her face and splattering over her light, dimming its brilliance as her helmet rolled away.

"Dang it." Her wrist throbbed where she'd tried to catch herself as she fell. She sat up and tried to wipe the dirt off her face, but the slick mud only smeared over her skin.

She should have been more careful. She should have paid more attention, but all she could think about was Jeremy…his lips…the way his body felt as it pressed against hers.

Blake grabbed her hard hat and wiped the dirt from its lamp. As the light brightened, it caught on something metal, sending a reflection against the far wall of the cave. She turned to find the object. There, at her feet, were the legs of a man.

The body was slumped forward and slightly to the side, propped against a rock. All of his clothes were in place, and if his skin wasn't gray and mottled, it was almost as if he could have simply fallen asleep. His feet were crossed loosely at the ankles, indicating that at the time of death he had been standing—she'd once heard it was because the left side of the brain shut down first and it caused the person's legs to cross as they fell, but whether it was that or simply inertia, she couldn't be sure. Yet, only those who were standing at the time of death fell as Robert had.

"Jeremy, stop," she called down the tunnel, but it was too late. Jeremy stepped into the light.

"Oh, my God," he whispered, looking down at the body. He moved his light, shining it on the man's face.

His skin was pale, mottled to the point of gray—the color of death. His eyes were open, but they were opaque and unseeing.

"Robert…" Jeremy illuminated the side of his brother's head.

There was a streak of dried, congealed blood down the side of his face and neck. His jacket was stained red and brown, and a pool of blood had settled and dried in his lap.

A gun was on the ground by his left hand. Next to the gun was a single spent casing.

One shot, one kill.

Jeremy dropped down to his knees as he stared at the man.

"Jeremy, you should go," she said. "I can take it from here."

"My brother…" Jeremy started, stunned. "This is my brother."

"I know. And he's always going to be your brother, but right now this is a crime scene."

Chapter Five

Jeremy wouldn't let her leave him outside the mine; instead he watched as she and her team documented the crime scene, taking measurements, pictures of the body and close-ups of Robert's face and the wound at his temple. They were doing their jobs, but it made his stomach churn every time he looked up and saw his brother's face.

Robert had had his fair share of issues, but Jeremy had never expected them to land them here—his brother dead and him watching as Robert's body was poked and prodded.

Blake looked to him as one of the investigators took a close-up of the bullet wound. "You okay? Are you sure you want to stay down here? It's been a long day."

"I'm fine."

She frowned, like she didn't believe him, but she didn't say anything. She turned to the other officer and handed him her camera. "Did they get a video?" Blake asked.

"Yep," the investigator answered.

"Great. Make sure to get some more pictures. Especially of the spatter."

The officer nodded, taking the camera. The strobing flash made Jeremy flinch, as if each picture was the crack of a bullet that had come too close.

He had to pull his crap together. For the next hour or so, he couldn't see the body as his brother if he wanted to get through this. This couldn't be Robert—it had to be just another face, or he'd never be able to be right again. And for dang sure, he didn't need Blake worrying about him. She needed to focus on her investigation.

He took a deep breath.

Blake took a swab of the body's hands. She tried to move his arm, but he was at full rigor. Leaning down, she sniffed his hands and then wrapped them in paper bags.

"You smell anything?" he asked, glancing down to the place where the handgun rested.

"Hard to say," she said with a slight shrug. "His hands smell heavily of dirt. That can cover the scent of powder."

He nodded.

"You want to take a sniff?" she asked, motioning to the bagged hands.

If this was his scene, he would have done

it, but he still couldn't let go of the fact it was Robert. No matter how badly he wanted to, he couldn't feel his brother's cold, lifeless flesh.

"I'm good, but make sure you're getting everything." He pointed at Robert's underarms. "Did you get a picture of his coat? How it's bunched up where someone would have put their hands if they were dragging him."

Blake frowned like she didn't agree, but she motioned to the officer taking pictures. "Make sure we get a picture of that."

The man nodded, his camera flashing.

"After the coroner's done, I want you to bag that gun and send it off to the crime lab. I want prints pulled and a ballistics test. Got it?"

"No problem," the officer said between pictures.

She turned to Jeremy. "You know I'm sorry about your brother and everything that's going on in your life right now, but that doesn't mean you can come in and tell me how to run a crime scene."

That's not what he had implied, but apparently he had hit a sore spot. "Right."

She pulled off her blue gloves with a snap and turned to the other investigator. "You done?"

The officer nodded, handing her camera to her. "I think we've got everything you'll need." He started down the tunnel, leaving Blake standing alone with Jeremy.

She stood up and brushed off her knees. "Don't worry, Jeremy. Even though it's just little ol' me in charge, we can figure out what happened."

OUTSIDE THE TUNNEL, Blake set the camera on the table at the makeshift command post and she tried to control her breathing. The vic may have been Jeremy's family, but that didn't mean that he could come in and try to tell her how to do her job. She never should have let him trail along. She should have trusted her gut and kept her distance.

The industrial lights made the night as bright as midday. Jeremy sat outside the mine's entrance as a few other officers milled through the grass and brush looking for any other evidence. The coroner walked down the trail from Robert's driveway, and she gave him an acknowledging wave.

She flipped through her camera, looking at the different photos of Robert's body, the gun and the walls in and around the scene. The last picture was of the blood spatters on the wall behind the body. The spray had moved far in the chasm, but the heaviest was just to the right of where Robert had slumped.

She made a note in her investigation report as the coroner stopped beside her.

"Have a dead one, eh? Lucky for you, the state's hotel is always open," he said, trying to make a joke. She didn't find it funny.

Blake nodded in Jeremy's direction. "That's the vic's brother, so be careful what you say."

The older man's flabby, jovial face turned placid. Most coroners were former police officers and more of the quiet type, but this one had come out of Wyoming and seemed to live for his job.

"Got it. So what do you think? Suicide?" He looked over her shoulder at the camera. "Oh, that's some nice spatter."

She put the camera down and out of sight of the death-happy coroner. "Right now I'm unsure. It's presenting like a suicide, no drag marks."

"Hmm…" The coroner made a note. "Anything else?"

"The vic had a bullet wound to the left side of his head."

"Was the vic left-handed?"

She hadn't thought to ask Jeremy. "I don't know."

The coroner nodded. "Well, I'll see what I can make of it."

"Sounds great, thanks. My investigator will take you to the body." She pointed to the other officer, who motioned for the coroner to follow him.

The coroner talked constantly as he and the other man made their way into the mine.

She opened her computer and pulled up her investigation report. Based on the rate of algor mortis, rigor mortis and livor mortis, the man had been dead approximately twelve hours. She looked at her watch. That put time of death at a little before noon, but the family hadn't been able to contact him for several days. Was it possible that Robert had been trapped in the mine and, instead of waiting to asphyxiate, had chosen to take his own life? Or had there been others involved? Had someone collapsed the entrance of the mine in hopes of covering up a murder?

Robert was a recluse. If someone had wanted to murder him, hiding him in the mine was a hell of a way to take care of his body. If things had gone another way and his family hadn't reported him missing, he may never have been found.

She looked over at Jeremy. His head was in his hands and his shoulders were slumped; he looked broken. Guilt flooded her. She should have been more patient with him and his interference in her investigation—he'd only been trying to help. She walked over to him and put her hand on his shoulder. "I'm sorry."

He nodded but didn't look up.

"We're going to get to the bottom of this. Don't worry."

"I just don't understand it. Robert had problems, but…I never thought…"

She sat down next to him, their legs brushing. Though they barely touched, she hoped that her nearness brought him a small measure of comfort. "You and I both know that no one ever thinks this is going to happen. The only thing we can do for Robert now is to piece together how he ended up where he is."

Jeremy shifted slightly, like he was recoiling from the words…words he had no doubt said himself many times over.

"Do you know—was Robert left-handed?"

Jeremy nodded. "He could have done this to himself. But you know Robert...*knew* Robert," he said, correcting himself. "He wasn't the kind who'd do this. He was too angry. Too cynical. He lived to prove the world wrong."

They sat in silence as she watched the firemen pack up their gear and head out. Once in a while Jeremy would move like he was going to stand up, but he would quickly stop and sit back down.

Finally the coroner appeared at the mine's entrance and, spotting her, made his way over.

"What did you find?" she asked as they both stood up to greet him.

The coroner looked back as two men carried a black bag containing Robert's body out of the mine and toward the coroner's van. "You were right about the jacket, but I don't think he was moved. The lividity didn't point in that direction."

"You think it was a suicide?" Jeremy asked.

The coroner shook his head. "The stippling around the bullet's entrance wound was a little wider than what I normally see in cases of suicide, but it doesn't rule it out."

Blake moved to speak but Jeremy interrupted. "What about the spatter?"

"It's consistent with the body's presentation, but again, I think the gun was a little farther back at the time it was fired."

"So it's possible that he was murdered?" Jeremy asked, his voice filled with anger.

"Right now we know the cause of death is the gunshot wound, but until we get the medical examiner's findings, I'm ruling the manner of death as undetermined."

THERE WAS NOTHING worse than notifying the next of kin...especially when it was your own family. Jeremy had put it off as long as he could, waiting until the next afternoon, but his parents needed to find out before they heard the news from someone else in the small town.

He took a deep breath as he entered the pizza joint. It was full of families, and the roar of Skee-Ball from the game room in the back filled the air.

His family had been coming to this place since he was a kid. Everything from the red-and-white-checkered tablecloths to the hanging stained glass lights was the same. It even smelled the same—yeasty with a hint of garlic and overcooked dough. The place was nostalgic in all the wrong ways.

His parents were sitting at their regular booth, and he made his way over.

"Hiya, Jeremy," his mom said in an overly chipper voice.

He nodded and sat down next to her.

"Did you talk to Robert?" his father asked.

Maybe it had been an error to meet them in a public place to tell them about Robert's death, but at least this way they couldn't start fighting.

He picked up the napkin in front of him and started rolling the paper into little balls. "I saw him."

"Did you tell him that he needs to call his mother?" she asked, taking a dainty sip of her pop.

"Actually, I couldn't tell him anything." He laid the napkin to rest on the table. "Mom, Dad, I have some bad news."

"Is Robert in trouble again?" his father started. "I tell you, I'm going to have to sell our house to pay for his bail this time. He's got me about tapped out."

"He's not in jail." Jeremy ran his hands over

his face and looked up, across the table at his father. "Robert's dead."

His father's mouth hung open, and his mother turned to stone next to him. He instantly wished he had taken Blake's offer of coming along to tell his family. Maybe she could have softened the blow. Maybe the news would have been better coming from a woman. Yet, after their kiss, it felt like the only thing she wanted to do was get away from him. No, there was only him to impart the news of his brother's death.

"We found Robert's body. It's on its way to the Missoula Crime Lab for an autopsy. Right now the cause of death is unclear, but we should know soon."

"You don't know how he died?" his mother asked in a stunned whisper.

He put his arm around her and pulled her close. "He died instantly from a gunshot wound. Other than that, there's not much I can say."

He envisioned Robert's body slumped over. The gunshot to his head. The blood trickling down his neck, staining his shirt. He tried to blink the images away but failed.

His mother looked across the table at his father. "I told you that you should have gone out there sooner, Glen," she spat. "If you would have just listened."

"Veronica, this is hardly the first time Robert hadn't called us back. If I ran out there every time you wanted to, we'd practically live with him."

"If we had, maybe he wouldn't be dead." His mother started to cry. She pulled away from Jeremy's hug and ran out of the restaurant.

The *beep, beep, beep* of some video game in the back room echoed through his thoughts.

He had hoped things wouldn't have gone this way, but his parents would never change—they would forever live in a state of turmoil.

His father was staring at his hands. "Do you think he did it to himself?" he finally asked.

Jeremy shrugged. If he had to guess, the whole scene felt *off.* When most people committed suicide they left something to explain why, and normally there was some sort of indicator. Sure, Robert had been acting strange, but if he had been planning on suicide, he would have been getting rid of personal effects and saying his goodbyes—but none of that had happened.

Then again, maybe it was impromptu. Things with Tiffany were going to hell, so maybe he thought he could make her pay by taking his own life. But that didn't account for the mine entrance's collapse. Either there had been some kind of accident that had led to the collapse or someone else had been involved.

If he listened to his gut, someone had murdered his brother. He thought of Blake. She must have been thinking the same as he was.

"I don't know, Dad."

"Robert and I have had our fair share of problems, but just like you, he's my son… I need to know what happened."

"Don't worry, Dad. Come hell or high water, I'll get to the bottom of this. And if someone had a hand in his death, I'll make them pay."

Chapter Six

The next afternoon, Blake found herself standing in front of Detective Engelman's desk. While he talked on the phone, she stared at a stray bit of fuzz that was stuck to the graying stubble on his chin. The minutes ticked by. From the sour look that appeared on his face when he looked at her, this meeting couldn't be good.

Finally he hung up and turned to her.

"Thanks for waiting," he said, tenting his fingers in front of him on the desk. "I looked over the report you filed after last night's call."

She sat forward in her chair, readying herself for anything. "I took copious notes and documented everything. Was there a problem?"

He glanced over at his blank computer screen like he was expecting to see the report pulled up. "Why didn't you call me? You are a deputy, aren't you?"

She nodded.

"Look right there," he said, pointing to the brass nameplate that adorned his door. "What does that say?"

"Clark Engelman, detective," she recited.

"Exactly. If there is the possibility that a case may be a felony, it is your job to call me. I'm the detective in this county, not you...and not some guy from Missoula." He leaned back in his chair and put his hands behind his head. "It is your job to bring me in on cases like these."

"I'm sorry, sir, but this case hasn't been ruled a felony."

His face contorted with rage, but then it quickly disappeared, replaced by an air of dismissal. "Look, I understand how it is. You get to a scene. You find a body. Your adrenaline starts pumping. But that doesn't mean you get to skirt our policies and procedures. It is your job to notify me."

Something was happening here, something she couldn't put her finger on. Did he know something about this case that she didn't?

"You and I both know that the moment this case became a death investigation, you should have called me."

He was right, but in the cases of suicides, it wasn't a requirement that a detective be called in. With everything that had been happening, and with Jeremy involved, the thought of notifying Detective Engelman had slipped her mind. Apparently now there would be hell to pay.

There was a knock on the door behind her. "Clark?" Investigative Captain Prather asked, opening the door without waiting to be invited in. He looked to Blake and gave her an acknowledging tip of the head, as if he had expected to find her sitting in the hot seat.

"What is it, Captain Prather?"

"I'm glad I caught you both." He took a seat on the edge of the detective's desk and looked down on him. "I heard you had a bone to pick with West here over last night's vic."

Engelman looked slightly shell-shocked, and his hands balled into tight fists. "I—" he started to protest, but the captain cut him off with the wave of his hand.

He turned to her. "I just got done looking

over your investigation findings. No drag marks, eh?"

She shook her head. What game had she just become a pawn in? Things between the investigative captain and Detective Engelman were always tense. Most thought Engelman had only gotten the position thanks to the fact his brother was the mayor, but usually the two men in front of her did their best at hiding their indifference toward each other.

"Look," Detective Engelman started, "I will not be pushed out. I'm the damned detective here, not some little pissant deputy. If you were smart, she would be behind some desk, not working this investigation."

Blake stood up and slammed her fist down on the desk as she leaned into Engelman's face. "How dare you? I didn't ask to investigate this case. If anything, I did you a favor—"

"Don't say something you'll regret, West," the captain said, stopping her before she flew deeper into a rage. He gave her a sharp glance.

She slid her fists from the wood of the desk, letting them drop down to her sides. "Captain, I request that I be made lead investigator on the Lawrence case," she said robotically as she forced her anger from her voice.

The captain glanced at Engelman and nodded. "You have a bucketful of cases, isn't that right, Detective?"

"You have no reason… This is my… You can't just throw your weight around—my brother and his wife will hear about this," the detective stammered in argument.

"I look forward to chatting with your brother," the captain said. "Feel free to send him my way when you get the chance." Captain Prather stood up. "In the meantime, I want you to catch up on one of your many unsolved cases."

Blake muffled her laughter as Engelman glared at her.

"West, you come with me." The captain walked out into the hallway and she followed, closing the door behind them.

"West, you better do your best with this one," Prather said. "I'm sure it's clear how far I've stuck my neck out. Don't let the hatchet fall, or it will catch us both—got it?"

"Sir, how did you know that Engelman would be after me?" She motioned toward the detective's door.

"Let's just say I have an inkling that things aren't on the up-and-up with him. Let's leave it at that. Now, you get out there and do your job."

"I filed the search warrant to get into Robert's cabin this morning."

"Good. We need to get a handle on this case before the mayor has a chance to retaliate after he finds out that one of his boys won't be in the driver's seat."

BLAKE SAT IN her patrol car and stared at the search warrant that she'd been issued by the judge. She wasn't a detective. She hadn't meant to step on Detective Engelman's toes, and she damned sure didn't mean to start a war in the department. Yet here she was—stuck in the middle of a political battle and unsure of whom exactly she could trust.

Her mind went to Jeremy. He didn't have any real ties to her department. He couldn't be swayed by the politics that were going on just under the surface. Plus, he had a vested interest in the case. But that might cause more trouble than it was worth.

But somehow being around him calmed her. He was like a breath of fresh air after being stuck in the stuffy politics of a little town. If nothing else, he could be a consultant—Captain Prather had told her to do her best, and she could only do that with Jeremy's help. He could be a sounding board. With his help, she could handle this.

She thumbed the ridges on the steering wheel as she thought of the sexy detective and the way he always had a little bit of a five o'clock shadow.

If she asked him to be involved, he couldn't question her methods. This was her case. This was her chance to prove herself—and to show Engelman that she was just as good, if not better, than him at her job. If Jeremy was the man she thought he was, he would understand how important this case was to her.

Before she realized it, she was parked in front of Jeremy's parents' house. The historic brick home spoke to generations of miners past, of lives spent searching for something more. It stood in direct contrast to the stunted tree that formed a sort of fence between their property and her mother's.

She had leaned against that tree the first time she had been kissed. In the logic of a teenager, she had hoped that Jeremy would see, get jealous and finally make his move. But that had never happened. Instead, one kiss had led to another, and another, until suddenly she had fallen for Chuck Garnet, the boy from the wrong side of the tracks, and had been left pregnant and at her mother's mercy.

If only Jeremy had played by the rules she had set for him in her head.

She closed her eyes, and she was back in the

Foreman Mine, panicking. Pressed against the wall. Jeremy's warm breath on her cheek. His lips caressing hers.

Life could have been just like that moment—with Jeremy there to help her through her times of panic. To make her see sense when everything else seemed to be falling in on her. They could have been each other's everything.

Could they still?

No. That kiss had been a fluke. A man's attempt to stop a woman from losing her cool. He was helping her in the only way he knew how. No doubt it meant nothing to him. He was far too guarded, too linear, to want to get involved in her life. He had his own in Missoula.

There was a tap on her window, and she opened her eyes. Jeremy stood on the other side of the glass, looking at her. "What's up?"

he asked with a slight tip of the head. "Did you find out something?"

She shook her head as she rolled down the window. "Hey, get in. I need to run to your brother's place. Thought maybe you wanted to go with me," she said.

He got in the car.

She wasted no time. "How do you feel about working as a consultant on your brother's case?"

"I didn't think that was a question." Jeremy looked at her with a spark in his eye.

She wasn't sure if it was excitement or something else, so she quickly glanced away. If it was something else, it would only complicate things. As much as she wanted to kiss him again, it couldn't happen.

She clicked on the radio and let the country

music fill the tense air between them as they bumped down the road.

She darted a glance his way. Some of the color had returned to his face, and he looked better, less in shock than last night.

"You doing okay?"

He nodded and looked out the window and away from her. "How long you been a deputy?" he asked, changing the subject.

Although he looked okay, he must have been wrestling with what had happened, and she wasn't about to make him bring it back up.

"Just a few years. When were you promoted to detective?" Blake tried to ignore his cute half smile.

"I'm surprised that between my mother and your mother, you don't know all about me. Every time I call I get a full report on you."

He was right. Their mothers talked often and,

until the last year or so, she had been given the details of his life…all the way down to how his daughter was doing in school. Yet, after a while, it hadn't seemed right to be a passive bystander to his life, and she had asked her mother to stop telling her things.

"You don't think our mothers would be crazy enough to try and set us up, do you?" he continued with a laugh.

The laugh chased away the little puff of excitement she was feeling. He wasn't interested. And if he wasn't, then neither was she—at least as far as he could know.

"My mother knows well enough that I'd never date another cop. And I'm not one for long-distance relationships. Tried that before."

"Crashed and burned, huh?" he asked, a line of tension running through his voice, almost like he wanted to ask more.

"I've never been good at relationships. Long distance or otherwise."

Not even next door.

"I get what you mean." He looked away like he was drawing on a memory. "You ever think of getting married?"

Was he really grilling her on her thoughts on relationships because he cared, or was this just his awkward way of filling the time as they drove?

She pushed down the accelerator a little harder, forcing the patrol unit well past its comfort zone on the little dirt road that led out to the Foreman.

"I…uh…" she stammered, unsure how to answer his question.

"I get it. You are probably enjoying your single life."

"Do you?" she asked.

He shrugged. "Some days. Some days I miss being married."

The little wiggle of jealousy in her grew. She wasn't sure if she wanted to know about how much he missed his ex-wife. He'd had so much. Even though he was divorced, he'd been given a real chance at a relationship. He hadn't been stuck in a nowhere town, without a spouse, and living with his mother.

She was thankful to see the cabin approaching as they turned up Robert's driveway.

"Thinking about marriage, how long were Robert and Tiffany together?" she asked, avoiding the conversation that Jeremy seemed adamant to have.

"They've been on and off now for the last few years. I can't tell you exactly how long they were together, though—they eloped in

Vegas. Never told my mother. She was devastated when she found out."

"Where's Tiffany from?"

"I don't know…someplace in Southern California, I think. As far as I know, she's never been too stable. Moved around a lot."

She nibbled the inside of her cheek. If this woman was like Jeremy said, there was the possibility that they may never track her down. "The soul of a gypsy, huh?"

"I call it unstable."

So he was the kind who liked stability. Well, that she had in spades. She hadn't ever moved. Hadn't ever gone out and experienced the world. She was living the same life she'd always lived; she had just gotten older. Somehow her kind of stability didn't seem like what he was looking for.

"You try to find Tiffany yet?" he asked.

She nodded. "I've been trying her all morning. It's been going straight to voice mail. I couldn't find any numbers for her family."

Jeremy gave a light snort, as if he wasn't surprised. "They aren't much better than she is. From what I hear, they are the type that likes to live out of their car."

They'd need to find Robert's wife to notify him of his death, but there wasn't much more that she could do.

She pulled the car to a stop in front of the house and got out. Robert's cabin was cold as they posted the warrant and walked in. The place carried the scent of stale cooking, man and dryer sheets.

"You hear anything from the medical examiner?" Jeremy asked as she walked over toward the kitchen and stopped at the sink.

She shook her head.

"Don't you think you should have called them? Maybe we could get a better idea of what we need to be looking for."

"Look, Jeremy." She said his name as if it carried a pit. "I thought I made it clear to you when we were in the mine that I know what I'm doing. I don't need you, or anyone else, telling me how to do my job."

He stepped back as if her words were lashes. "Whoa. That's not what I meant," he said, putting his hands up like he was motioning for her to stop.

She wasn't a horse. She wouldn't be commanded.

"Then what did you mean? I'm tired of this. Just because I've only been a deputy for a couple of years, it doesn't mean I don't know how to function on a crime scene. It doesn't mean I don't know how to handle this investigation.

When the medical examiner is done, he will call. He doesn't need me telling him how to do his job."

Jeremy stepped forward and moved like he was going to take her hand, but then he stopped and just stared at her as if he was afraid she would bite.

"Look, I know how it is—how it always feels like you have to prove yourself, but you don't have to prove yourself to me."

She relaxed slightly. Hopefully he meant what he said. She couldn't fight him, too. She had enough battles on her hands.

"Sorry," she said with a sigh. "It's been a long day."

"What happened?"

She told him about her meeting in Detective Engelman's office. As she spoke, his face tightened.

"I'm so sick of this crap," he said, pressing his hand hard against the countertop as though he were squishing a bug. "I just dealt with something like this in Missoula."

She'd heard about it and had followed the story of a series of arsons that had led to the death of the battalion chief in Missoula's fire department and whispers of unanswered corruption. In the end, Jeremy had been called to the stand and forced to testify about the incident.

"I don't think this is the same thing. It's just normal politics—with a touch of nepotism."

"Oh, nepotism..." he said, rolling the word over his lips. "That never complicates a situation."

She chuckled. "Regardless, I'm glad to have you around. Get a fresh perspective on all this."

Her cheeks warmed as she thought about all the other reasons she liked having him around.

His sexy grin returned, as if he could read her mind.

She forced her thoughts back on the case. "As for what we're looking for, I filed the search warrant so we could locate your brother's financial and mining records. I thought that would be a strong place to start our work." She moved her weight from foot to foot as she tried to look at anything besides his smile. "Do you know where we could find them?"

He walked over to the pullout bed and lifted up the end. Packed underneath the metal frame were boxes overflowing with paperwork. "The last time I was here, he had some stuffed in the bathroom cabinets, as well," he said, pointing toward the only other room in the small space.

Blake grabbed one of the boxes from under

the bed and slid it out to the middle of the floor. There, on the top of the papers, was a letter from the county.

"Hey, take a look at this," she said, picking it up and reading its contents. "It looks like your brother has a tax lien." She handed him the certificate. "I think we have a clue as to why he may have wanted to commit suicide."

Chapter Seven

The word *suicide* left an ashy taste in Jeremy's mouth as he tried to swallow what Blake was saying. Robert wouldn't have committed suicide over some property tax lien. He wasn't the kind to roll over and just take a hit like that. He would have fought long and hard to protect what he had always called his "little corner of heaven."

He stared at the paper in his hand. According to the paperwork, the tax lien certificate was supposed to go to auction if his back taxes weren't paid. He looked at the date the letter had been issued. Three weeks ago. No doubt his brother had been worried about some company buying his lien and foreclosing on him.

It was just strange that his parents hadn't mentioned Robert's financial trouble. Robert must have been keeping it from them. Either he had the money and had intended on paying, or he had been trying to get it—without going to them. Maybe they were his last resort.

Jeremy shook his head. It didn't make sense. Something didn't feel right. "Let's keep looking. Maybe we can find more that will help us make sense of this."

Blake bent down. Her blond hair had started to wiggle loose from her tight ponytail, and a few stray locks fell into her face, making her look soft, touchable. For a moment he considered pushing the hair back from her face, but if he got that close again, it was hard to say what she would do. After what had happened between them in the mine, it was likely that she would get upset—and he couldn't risk his chance at having a hand in solving his brother's case.

Family came first, no matter how badly he wanted Blake…or how badly he had wanted her ever since they were in high school.

She pushed the hair out of her face, annoyed. "Your brother needed a better filing system," she said, pulling a stack of papers out of the box and setting them on the floor.

The hair fell loose again, and this time he turned away. He couldn't think of her like that…like anything other than a childhood friend or, better yet, a colleague.

He sat down on the floor next to her and started shuffling through the receipts, bills and pamphlets. They worked for at least an hour. No matter how badly he wanted to concentrate, all he could seem to focus on was the way her arm bumped against his as they each shuffled through the papers. Why couldn't his brother have lived in a house that was something a little bigger than a glorified garage?

"Have you found anything?" He leaned toward her, his arm grazing hers as he looked into the pile of papers she had sitting in her lap.

She flipped through the pages. "Not much, but your brother did seem to keep a constant record of his copper sales." She lifted up a receipt that had a four-figure number circled at the bottom. "Do you think that is his haul for a month or a year?"

Jeremy shrugged. "Hard to say. Let's make a pile though. See if we can track his income."

He picked up his stack of papers and scanned through them, pulling out any possible income sources that Robert had in the last year. As he worked, Blake's nearness became less uncomfortable.

The income stack grew and started to spill over. Jeremy picked it up and began to add the numbers in his head. "Just looking at these," he said, picking up the stack and straightening it, "Robert had to have pulled in more than a hundred thousand dollars last year. I'm sure he had some sizable expenses, but that seems more than enough to pay the taxes on his property."

Blake looked up at him. "I haven't seen much in the paperwork to indicate that he had any significant form of debts—but maybe his outgo was in another box."

Jeremy reached under the bed and grabbed the next box. He opened the lid and threw it to the floor.

"Oh…" he said, staring at the pile of women's panties and bras. On top was a folded purple lace thong. He grabbed the lid to hide the box's contents.

"What is it?" Blake asked, peeking over. "Oh…" She giggled, the sound that cute noise between embarrassed and amused.

The pink hue of her cheeks darkened into full red as she blushed. She looked young, vibrant, as the color moved through her features and all the way into her ears. She reached over and picked up the panties. They unfurled in her long fingers.

"Something tells me that these probably aren't in Robert's size." She laughed, dropping them back into the box. "He and Tiffany must have been having a good time…at least at some point."

For a moment, as he looked at her, he thought of her wearing those purple panties and a bra to match. In his daydream, she was sauntering toward him, her curves bouncing ever so slightly, teasing him as she moved.

"It's funny. I think I have the same pair in blue," she joked, winking at him. "In fact, I might be wearing them now." She reached down and unclipped her utility belt and carefully let it fall to the floor. Peeling back the waistband of her pants, she revealed the top of her panties. "No, they're cotton. But they are magenta," she said with a laugh. "So close to sexy, but so far."

"Hey, I think cotton can be sexy," he said, wishing he could have seen more. He suddenly felt a little more at ease than he had before.

Her giggle returned. "Then you would love my bra. I think it's even beige. You haven't seen sexy until you've seen me in a nude-colored cotton bra and mismatched panties."

"Oooohhh, baby." He fanned himself as he laughed.

He liked this side of her, the relaxed, play-ful and unlocked version of herself that he had never seen. He started to tell her. He stopped out of fear that if he said it, she would close up and the little spark he was seeing would fade away.

"You've seen mine," she teased, motioning to her panties. "It's only fair if I see yours."

He tried to stop the lust that rose in his core. Dang, Blake was sexy.

He stood up and walked over to the radio, then flicked it on. A Bob Seger CD clicked to life, and the song "Night Moves" filled the air.

"What are you doing?" Blake asked with a playful frown. "Are we having a little Throwback Thursday thing here?"

"First, it's not Thursday. And, second, I happen to like Bob Seger. Or at least I did when I was a kid," he said with a chuckle.

"I bet you're a Billy Ray Cyrus fan, too, huh?"

He started to sing "Achy Breaky Heart."

"Oh, my God, please stop. Once that song gets in your head it never leaves," she said, moving her hands up like she was guarding herself from his singing.

"Come on. I'm not that bad of a singer, am I?"

She looked up at him with a twinkle of glee in her eye. "If I were you, I would stick to being a detective."

He lunged toward her like a teenager, unthinking as he pulled her into his arms and growled. "How dare you?" he teased as her breath caressed his cheek.

She put her arms around him. As her chest pushed into his, he could feel her heart hammering. Suddenly he realized how close they were, how she felt like she belonged in his arms—more, in his life. Everything just felt so good. So natural. So real.

He leaned in, kissing her lips. They were welcoming and firm, echoing his own needs and fears. She kissed him back, their tongues moving against each other, waking every nerve ending in his body.

She ventured closer, forcing him down to the hard floor as she moved atop him. Blake sat up, pressing her warmth against him, gently rocking as she teased his responding body. He reached down, taking hold of her hips, slipping his thumbs under the edge of her uniform top. As his cold fingers touched her hot flesh, she went still and just stared at him.

He wished he could know what she was thinking. Then again, it probably wasn't too hard to guess. She was probably wondering if this was the right decision. If this was the right time. If it was a bad idea to take things down this road with him.

What they were doing was wrong for so many reasons. They were in his brother's house searching for clues about his death, but if Robert's death had taught him anything it was that he couldn't let moments like these pass him by. Life was too short to play by the rules. This moment—holding her in his hands and feeling the warmth of her breath against his skin—this was right.

He pushed his thoughts aside. Blake was the kind who took what she wanted. And he was eager to give it.

BLAKE LOOKED DOWN at him, the way his muscular chest pulled against his T-shirt, accentuating the lines of his pecs. How had they gotten here at a time like this?

She stopped herself. They were working, but it didn't matter. All that mattered was that her fantasy, the thing she'd wanted forever was happening.

His thumb caressed her skin, his touch reassuring but at the same time making her core warm and her belly stir. He wanted her. He looked at her with his piercing green eyes; in their depths she could see a gleam that spoke of carnal appetite.

Had he been without sex as long as she had? From the way she instinctively rolled her hips, her body hadn't forgotten how glorious it could be—and how good it could be with Jeremy.

Reaching down, she lifted the edge of his shirt and let her fingers trace the waistband of his jeans. There was a fine line of dark hair that trailed down, disappearing under his clothes. She wished she could follow that line, all the way down to—

He sat up, breaking her wandering thoughts. When she thought he would step back from her and end this sensual assault, he leaned in and kissed her again. This time his kiss was deeper, headier than the last. She could taste his flavor, salty, sweet and faintly minty. He tasted so good, and she sucked at his lips, pulling the bottom one into her mouth.

He moaned, the sound deep and throaty, hungry.

She pushed him back, gently but firmly, and slid her hands down and unbuttoned his pants.

"Boxers kind of guy?" she teased, pulling at the elastic band of his red flannel underwear.

"I'm just like you. I'm a cotton man."

"My favorite kind of guy." She laughed. "I don't know what I would have done if you were wearing a G-string."

He laughed, and as he moved his body shifted under her. He pressed hard against her, making her nearly forget what they had been laughing about. All she could focus on was the way he felt under her and all the things she could do with his reacting body.

She moved off him to between his legs. Ever so slowly, she edged down his pants, kissing his skin as she pulled them lower and lower down his thighs.

His pheromone-laced scent nearly made her mouth water as she kissed over the cloth at the intersection of his legs and groin. He tensed under her touch, and she felt him come to life beneath her lips. Much as she didn't want to, she stopped. He needed to want her more than he had ever wanted anyone before. She wanted him to beg her to let him have her. She would take her time in seducing him, pushing him to the edge and reeling him back in, again and again.

The pants thumped as they hit the floor. But that was not the sound that stopped her. It was her phone. Vibrating loudly, it started to ring.

"I better answer that," she said, a bit breathless.

He nodded, but his face fell with disappointment.

She stepped away from him and grabbed the phone. "This is West."

"I'm calling in reference to Robert Lawrence." It was the medical examiner, Les Taver.

The man had always been short on frivolities, but maybe that was what happened when you worked with the dead all day.

"I'm glad to hear from you, Les. What's going on?"

"After performing a full autopsy, I've made a ruling in Robert's death. It's a homicide."

Chapter Eight

Falling into Jeremy's arms had been a mistake. One Blake couldn't repeat. He was off-limits for so many reasons. Not the least of which was his brother's murder. Now that she had a homicide on her hands, anything between them could be seen as a conflict of interest. She couldn't risk being pulled off the case because of her feelings toward him. She had promised the captain she would do her best to solve this case, and a relationship with Jeremy would only jeopardize everything.

She slid her belt back on and clipped it into

place. "Put your pants back on, Jeremy," she said, her voice riddled with an air of forced indifference.

He opened his mouth to say something, but she shot a look at him. "That was the medical examiner. He's ruled your brother's death a homicide."

Jeremy stood up and threw his clothes back on, jumping around as he pushed his legs into his jeans. "I knew it."

She tried to stop herself from feeling the urge to watch as Jeremy zipped his pants.

He looked at her, measuring her in a glance. "What did the examiner find?"

"He said that there wasn't any gunpowder on Robert's hands. He couldn't have fired the gun."

She looked down at her phone. "He said he was going to email me his findings. It sounds like there was also some kind of note."

"A note?"

"Your brother had put it inside the waistband of his pants. Maybe it was his way of sending us a clue."

She nodded as her phone buzzed to life. She clicked on the email from the medical examiner. "It's here."

The handwritten note was slightly grainy, but she could easily make out the words as she read.

To whoever's gonna read this letter,

The moment before lightning strikes, electricity fills the air. Metal vibrates and rings. Hair stands on end. The only thing a miner can do is lie down and pray. Pray violently. Pray like you ain't never prayed before. Then you wait for the moment that a million volts strike...and you hope that death doesn't find you.

Until now, I always thought my biggest fear was lightning, that I would be struck down, a pickax in my pack and a shovel in my hand. I realize now what a fool I have been. It wasn't lightning I should have feared. I shouldn't have feared the earth. I should have feared my fellow man. If I had paid more attention, I would have known that the thing I love most would be the death of me.

Robert Lawrence

What did the letter mean?

Jeremy walked over and stood beside her, staring at her phone. "The thing I love most," he read aloud. "What did he love the most?" he asked rhetorically, tapping his fingers against his bottom lip.

Sitting on the floor, beside the box, was the

tax lien paperwork. "Do you think he meant the land? Maybe his mine?"

Jeremy nodded. "Absolutely, but why would someone want to kill him for it?"

She picked up the financial papers. "Look at this. He's been making money hand over fist. Maybe someone found out. Someone who wanted what he had. Money and love are the most common motivators in a murder."

He handed her back her phone, and she slipped it into her pocket. "Who issues a tax lien?"

"In this case, it was the county. I think the county treasurer holds it until it's paid or it goes to auction."

The blood drained from her face as she remembered the name of the treasurer.

"What's the matter?" Jeremy asked, taking her by the arm like he was afraid she would faint.

"I...I know him."

"Who? The treasurer?"

She nodded, her body stiff and numb with realization. "His name's Roger Davy."

"Okay." Jeremy frowned. "What does that mean?"

"Roger Davy is the mayor's brother-in-law. Detective Engelman is his brother..." She forced herself to take a breath. "What if the mayor has something to do with this?"

She had to have it all wrong. Just because her leads pointed toward the Engelman family didn't mean that a corrupt system was behind this murder. She had to be missing something.

But if she was right, she was in over her head.

Had this been what Captain Prather was hinting at? Why he'd wanted her to take the case—because he knew she didn't have a connection to that family? Was he setting her up to take a fall or to find the truth?

She had to sit down.

"It's possible…but why? What would the mayor want from my brother?" Jeremy's eyes turned dark, and she could have sworn she saw a shadow of hatred in them.

She shrugged. "I don't know. But maybe they filed the lien and then had to keep Robert from paying it. He must have had enough money, or at least access to enough. If he couldn't pay his tax lien, then anyone could buy his land. They could take the property for just a few thousand bucks."

"Does that give them the mineral rights, as well?"

"I don't know for sure," Blake said. "But probably, if it's all on the same deed."

"Just because these men are related doesn't mean that they're in it together. I mean, why would the mayor put himself into a compromising position?"

"Most of these tax liens are bought out by holding or investment companies."

"So?"

"The largest investment company in the county is Tartarus Environmental Investments. And who do you think the CEO is?"

Jeremy shook his head.

"The one and only Mayor John Engelman."

"This is still only circumstantial evidence. There's nothing that directly ties the mayor to Robert's death."

"Not yet, but I have a feeling if we just look hard enough, we'll find what we're looking for."

"Hold on." Jeremy leaned against the back of the couch. "We need to proceed slowly. Let's not jump to any conclusions."

Maybe Jeremy was right. She needed to slow down. If she had this wrong, there would be fallout.

"We need to get this evidence back to the unit," she said, staring at the papers strewn over the floor.

"First we need to make sure we have pictures of everything. If what you are saying is true, there's a good chance something could disappear."

She made sure to get a clear picture of every piece of paper she thought could be of any use in their investigation. Then they dropped the boxes of paperwork off with the evidence unit.

As they drove away from the office, Blake called the captain.

"West, how's it going?" Captain Prather asked.

She told him about the medical examiner's findings and the connection between Engelman and Davy. The captain was silent for several moments.

"Dang it," he said finally in a muted whisper. "Do you have any direct evidence?"

"No, sir."

"Then don't you dare utter a word of this to anyone else. If you're wrong, this could cost us both our jobs."

"I know, sir." She paused, then, "Sir, do you have the number for the mayor's PA? I was hoping that maybe I could talk to them and at least get a line on the mayor's whereabouts at the time of Robert's death."

He rattled off a number.

She tapped it into her phone.

"West," Captain Prather continued, "you better hope that you're wrong. This kind of thing could bring everything down on top of the entire county."

"What exactly do you mean, sir?" She wasn't sure, but she could have sworn from the tone of his voice that he was suddenly regretting ever putting her on this case.

"Nothing, West. Just tread softly."

The phone line went dead.

She looked to Jeremy, who was sitting in the passenger's seat, his head in his hands. He must have heard everything. "Heck of a way to spend your days off from your department, isn't it?"

"It looks like I may need to take a few more days off," he said, forcing a smile.

She started to reach over to take his hand but stopped. Something about touching him seemed wrong. They had already taken things too far. They couldn't do that again. It could compromise everything—their friendship, her investigation and even her job. And if the mayor was involved, as she assumed, it was hard to tell how far those political ties went.

Montana was a large state, but when it came to connections and secrets, sometimes it was entirely too small. Both of them could be in danger.

She had to call the mayor's personal assistant. She had to eliminate the mayor and his cronies from her list of suspects. They couldn't possibly have been involved. They didn't get to where they were by being stupid and getting mixed up in homicides—at least ones that would point directly to them.

She dialed the number the captain had given to her, and the mayor's PA answered.

"This is Deputy Blake West. I was hoping to catch up with the mayor today. Do you know where he is?" she asked, trying to avoid the question she most desperately wanted to ask.

"He's in Helena today with his wife. He

should be back tomorrow morning. Can I let him know you called?"

"No," she said, maybe a bit too emphatically. "No," she repeated, this time a little softer. "It's fine. By chance, when did they leave for Helena?"

The PA was quiet for a moment. "Well, he had the finals for the Montana Shooting Sports Championship here in Butte this week, so he had to wait until this morning to leave, but his wife is set to arrive in Helena this evening."

A gun championship? If Engelman had been competing, then he may have an airtight alibi for his whereabouts at the time of Robert's death.

"Oh, I heard the about the championships," Blake lied as she tried to draw the PA into a conversation in which she could learn more. "How did Mayor Engelman do?"

The PA laughed. "Oh, he wasn't shooting. He was just making an appearance. Anything for a little publicity and a few bucks, you know."

The knot in her gut tightened. "I see."

"Is there something you wanted to talk to him about?" the PA asked.

An edge of panic cut through her. No one else could catch wind of her investigation or where it was pointing—especially not the mayor.

"No, but thanks."

"Are you sure?" the PA pressed, her voice flecked with suspicion.

"Yes. I'll try and get in touch with him later. Our department was just wondering if he would be available later this month. We're working on a public event," she lied, trying to cover her tracks.

"Oh, okay." The warmth returned to the PA's voice. "I'm sure he'd be interested."

"Great, just great," Blake said, the panic returning to her voice. "Talk to you soon." She hung up the phone.

Blake's feint had worked, but there would be no guarantees for how long. It had been a bad idea to call the PA. Now her name would be on the mayor's radar. And if he was responsible in any way, he would be alerted to the possibility that he was under investigation. She let out a ragged breath.

"What's the matter?" Jeremy asked, staring at her.

She tried to shake off the thoughts that plagued her. "Nothing. No worries."

"I know you. You can't lie to me."

Was that true? Did he really *know* her? She had been on her own for so long now that she balked at the thought that a man—no, not just some man, but Jeremy—really cared enough to think that he *knew* her. She looked at him for a moment, taking in the barely noticeable crow's feet that adorned his perfectly almond-shaped eyes. Eyes that seemed to look straight through her. Eyes that seemed to see her for who she really was, and not the hard-edged person she tried to show to the world.

She looked away. She couldn't fall for those eyes, or the man behind them. She couldn't let herself lose her focus or her edge.

"I think I got a lead," she said, skirting the issue. "Mayor Engelman was at the Shooting Sports Championship."

"That's not much of a lead."

"No, but we have a solid place to start investigating our number one suspect."

Chapter Nine

At the gun range men and women were standing in the trapshooting fields, and the sharp echoes of shotgun blasts and the scent of spent gunpowder filled the air. In a strange way, the smell of the powder made Blake comfortable. She'd spent so many days on the range with her standard-issue Glock 22 .40 caliber pistol. Every officer in combined city and county sheriff's office, known as the Butte–Silver Bow County Sheriff's Department, had been issued the same gun, but over time hers had become special. It had become a part of her. She reached down and touched its familiar grip.

She and Jeremy made their way to the clubhouse. A man in his early twenties sat behind the counter reading a *Guns & Ammo* magazine. He looked up as they approached.

"How can I help you, Officer?" he asked, setting the magazine down on the counter and giving them his full attention.

She smiled. "I was just wondering about yesterday's competition. Was the mayor here?"

"Yeah," the clubhouse manager said with a sharp nod. "Mayor Engelman gave a great speech on the need for enforcing our Second Amendment rights."

"How long was the competition?"

"The prelims started last week. Yesterday was the finals." He rambled on about the winners and their shooting averages, while Blake pretended to listen.

"Was the mayor here the entire time?" Jeremy asked when the man took a break between statistics.

The manager nodded. "He was here on and off throughout the week, and yesterday he was here most of the day. Made a big thing out of it. You should have seen it—he even took a turn on the shooting stage. Missed just about all the clays, but you know how it is, not being his gun and all."

"He's not a good shot?" Jeremy asked, giving her a questioning look.

The manager passed them a grin. "Hey, I ain't saying he's bad. He just ain't a shotgun man."

If the mayor wasn't a good shot with a shotgun, it didn't mean that he wasn't necessarily a good shot with a handgun—particularly the one that had been used in Robert's murder. Heck, anyone could have been a good shot at such close range. Then again, would the mayor really have wanted to get his hands dirty? Would the glad-handing, speech-making, baby-kissing mayor really be capable of pulling a trigger to get something he wanted?

Jeremy laughed. "Hey, we can't all be good at everything. Am I right?" he asked, chumming up with the club's manager.

"Hey, I heard he's real good with a sidearm."

"Is that right?" Blake asked, perking up.

"That's the talk around the clubhouse. I had a guy in here yesterday. Said he was shooting with the mayor just last week. He said the guy could shoot a solid grouping at twenty-one feet."

"Who was the guy the mayor went shooting with?" Jeremy asked as he leaned against the counter in what she assumed was his attempt to look nonchalant and nonconfrontational—anything to put the manager at ease and make him talk a little more. It was enthralling to watch Detective Lawrence in action, the way he looked at the man like he was a friend rather than a source feeding them much-needed information.

"I think the guy's name was Todd. Maybe Todd O'Banyon or something."

"O'Banyon?" Blake asked. "Do you mean O'Brien? Todd O'Brien?" *Robert's neighbor.*

"That sounds about right. The mayor and Todd were in the bar," he said, motioning over to the door on the other side of the clubhouse, which must have led to the tavern. "Todd had a few beers after the mayor left, and then he finally stopped talking about what good friends they were. He was thinking himself some kind of big man. I think maybe the mayor even bought a gun off of him."

"Do you know what kind of gun?" Blake asked.

The man shrugged. "Some kind of Glock. I don't remember. Like I said, the guy had a few beers under his belt. From what I heard, it's possible that he was just making it all up."

"What do you mean?" Jeremy's body tensed, but the manager didn't seem to notice.

"I don't know. The guy was just talking all kinds of nonsense—about how he was going to be a millionaire if he played his cards right. You know. Crazy talk."

Had they gotten it all wrong? Was O'Brien the man they were looking for? Or was he involved in the mayor's plot? Why would the mayor be buying a gun from someone—especially Robert's neighbor?

"Did he mention how he was going to be making these millions?" Jeremy asked, a cold edge to his voice.

The man shifted in his chair. "I dunno," he said with a shrug. "It was Greek to me. Something about buying investment properties or something."

She thought back to Todd O'Brien's property. It was covered with rusted-out car frames and filled with garbage. How could a man who couldn't afford the upkeep for his property afford to invest? Todd O'Brien had never had a job, as far as she knew.

"Is there something I should know about?" the clubhouse manager asked.

Jeremy shook his head. "Nah, it's no big thing. We're just looking into a few different things. If necessary, though, would you mind if we came back and asked you a few more questions?"

The manager smiled. "Not at all. I appreciate all that you guys do. You have the hardest job of anybody, protecting the streets. The least I can do is answer a few questions."

Sometimes she loved living in Montana, where law enforcement officers—for the most part—were treated with respect. It wasn't the same everywhere else. She read about it in the national headlines all the time, officers being shot or their homes vandalized simply because of the job they were drawn to do. And those in her profession were constantly struggling with the stigma of being crooked.

She thought of the mayor. Maybe he was part of the problem. There were always a few in public service who were corrupt. It was the political way. Unfortunately, across the country it was her brethren who had to pay.

JEREMY FLIPPED THROUGH the saved pictures on Blake's camera as he waited. He scrolled past the images of Robert's body and stopped at the picture of the gun that sat next to his brother's hand. It was the standard police-issued Glock.

Every fiber of his being told him that this gun was the same one the manager had told them about. Instant hatred flooded his veins. The mayor was likely behind his brother's death. Now he and Blake would just have to prove it.

He looked over at Blake, who was having the clubhouse manager sign a statement. The man had taken the questioning remarkably well. In Missoula, things were a little tenser with the public—especially after the strings of arsons and his involvement in the investigation. He and his department were still trying to win back the public's trust.

It was hard to know who to trust anymore, and the public felt the same way. In a world full of lies and corruption, few stood above it; few wanted to live with honor.

He looked back at the photos on the camera and started scrolling through them. He came to the ones they'd taken earlier, at Robert's house. Some of the documents in the photos were ones that Blake had gone through, and he hadn't seen them. Now he took his time, scanning through them. He clicked again. On the screen was a picture Blake had taken of a photograph in Robert's files; it was of a car parked in Todd's driveway. The date marked on the photograph put it at having been taken a week ago.

Why would Robert have taken a picture of a random car and then slipped it into his files? He must have wanted to keep it as a record of something, but what?

The picture was dated one week prior to his brother's death.

He zoomed in on the license plate. It was the

blue vanity plates that celebrated Glacier National Park. He made note of the number.

After picking up his phone, he called Dispatch. A woman answered, and he gave her his information. "I need to run a plate," he said, reciting the number.

There was a long pause as the dispatcher clicked away in the background. After a moment she came back. "The license plate is for a 2015 silver Land Rover registered to John Engelman. Is there anything else you'd like to know, sir?"

His breath wheezed from his lungs. "No, thanks," he said, forcing the words from his body.

His brother had left him a sign. He had left Jeremy the evidence he needed to bring the sucker to his knees.

Chapter Ten

The ride back to their houses was tense. How could she have missed the picture of the mayor's car? Jeremy's face was tight as he stared out the window. Whether he was angry or just preoccupied with the details of the case, Blake couldn't be sure.

Hopefully he didn't think she was incompetent. She was working this case as fast as she could, and sometimes things fell through the cracks, but that didn't mean she didn't care. If anything, she cared about this case more than she should. Most of the time, even when she knew the victims, she could gain emotional distance—but not this time, not when the vic was Jeremy's brother.

Maybe she was too close. It had certainly been a mistake to find herself on the floor with Jeremy. It had been so exciting, so euphoric to be wanted by him, to be in his arms and desired, but she shouldn't have let down her guard. It had added a degree of tension to everything they did, every expression he made—like now.

As soon as she parked he got out of the car and slammed the door.

"Wait," she called as she went after him. "What's your problem?"

He looked surprised as he turned back.

Had her insecurities made her jump to conclusions? Was he not really upset with her? She instantly regretted her tone.

"What?" he asked.

"What's going on with you, Jeremy?" she asked, trying in another way to see if she was crazy or not.

He frowned. "Nothing."

That was a cop-out. Everything about him, from the way his eyes had darkened to the way that even now his body turned from her like he was desperate to run away, said otherwise. "Don't lie to me, Jeremy."

He turned to face her. "There's nothing wrong," he said, his voice hard and his words abrupt.

Blake walked toward him so they were toe-to-toe. "You don't get to be angry with me. You missed that picture, too. If nothing else, it's just good that we found it. Now we have evidence—"

"That's not it," he said, looking toward her house.

She followed his gaze. The lights were off inside, but that didn't mean that her mother wasn't watching. She turned her back to the windows. "Then what is it, Jeremy? Are you mad about what happened at your brother's? If that's the case, it won't happen again. It was a mistake in the first place."

He took her by the arms and looked into her eyes. "Stop. I'm not upset with you."

"Then why are you so pissed? Why have you barely spoken to me since the range?"

He looked toward his parents' house. "I'm not pissed. I'm just... I'm just... I don't know. Look. Here's the deal. In a few minutes, I'm going to have to walk in there," he said as he motioned toward his parents' house. "And I'll have to tell them that we don't have a suspect in Robert's case. They are going to want to know everything the medical examiner said and what we've done. It's going to be brutal."

"You don't have to tell them anything," she said, softening under his touch.

"You know that isn't realistic. If you think your mother's bad, imagine what she'd be like if something happened to you."

She shuddered at the thought. Her mother would be distraught. As much as they got under each other's skin, they were everything to each other.

"My mother is more upset than I've ever seen her." He rubbed his thumb over the fabric of her uniform. "The worst part of it all is that I don't know what to do. I've never been good at that sort of thing. I don't know the right words."

"Just listen to your heart and be honest." As the words fell from her lips, she couldn't help but feel like a hypocrite. Here she was telling him to be honest, to follow his heart, but that was the last thing she was going to do. She couldn't tell him how she felt…how she had always wanted him. It was too big of a risk, putting her trust in someone else.

"I—" He stopped.

"What were you going to say?" That little part of her heart that held all her desires sprang to life with the hope he would say what she wanted to hear—he wanted her and they could be together.

He let go of her arms and stepped back from her. The way he moved made it seem as though he wasn't putting just physical distance between them but emotional distance, as well.

"I appreciate what you're doing, Blake," he said, his hard-edged voice in direct opposition to the softness of his words. "I mean with the investigation and all. You're doing everything you can."

She waited for the "but."

"But," he continued as the single word made her heart sputter and her fingers go numb, "what we did at Robert's…you were right. What happened was a mistake. I have only been divorced for a little over a year. I know that seems like a long time, and I would be okay, but I have my daughter to think about."

She nodded, not sure if she could handle standing there and listening to what she knew was coming.

"I'm sure you feel the same way," he said.

He couldn't have understood the way she was feeling right now—the way she wanted to run away, to crawl under her sheets and hide. Still, another part of her wanted to stand up and tell him he was wrong—that they could have it all, that they could be together. That they could figure it out if they both loved each other enough.

Love. The word dropped like a stone in a bucket. It rippled through her, the weight of its meaning cascading all the way down to her toes. That was the problem. Neither of them could have love.

There was no room left in their hearts.

BLAKE SAT ON the edge of Megan's bed and stroked her daughter's damp blond hair. She smelled like lavender shampoo and innocence.

"Get some sleep, pumpkin." She leaned down and gave her a kiss on the forehead and then she turned and slipped the book back onto the shelf, next to her daughter's well-loved red-headed doll, one of the mementos she'd kept from her childhood.

"Mom, wait," Megan called just as she moved to stand up.

"What, honey?"

"Mom," Megan said, her voice smooth but laced with sleepiness. "Are you going to ever get married?"

The question came out of left field and forced Blake to slump back onto Megan's bed. "What do you mean? Where did that come from?"

"Well, Grandma was on the phone today and she was talking about Jeremy. She said that she hoped you'd get married to a man like him." Megan took her hand; her skin was warm and soft. "Do you love him?"

Why did her mother have to put ideas like this into Megan's head? There was no right answer. No matter what she said, Megan would riddle her with more questions—questions that a thirteen-year-old didn't need to ask. She just needed to enjoy being young and not worrying about her mother's romantic relationships—or lack thereof.

She thought of Jeremy and where they had left things with each other. Maybe he had been right in pushing her away with the excuse that they needed to think of their children first. If things were like this, confused and up in the air, the last thing she wanted to do was involve Megan. Above anything else, her daughter needed to be protected.

"Pumpkin, I love *you*." She pushed a hair off Megan's slightly sweaty neck.

"I know, Mom, but it would be kind of cool, you know…"

"What do you mean?"

"Well, I don't know," Megan said, skirting around what she wanted to say. "I guess it would be just kind of cool if I had a dad. I mean a dad I actually saw and stuff. Think about it. I could even have a sister if you married Jeremy. It would be so fun."

She didn't want to burst Megan's illusion by telling her that in real life, relationships weren't that simple. They were just another method through which you could get hurt.

"We don't need a man in our lives just to make us happy, pumpkin. Women are so strong. We can do anything," she said, flexing her arms as she tried to make light of the multiple layers of her daughter's innocent but pain-inducing words.

"Oh, I know you're strong, Mom." Megan waved her off. "But he makes you smile. I like it when you smile. You look beautiful."

"Not as beautiful as you." She wanted to take her daughter by the arms and tell her that she wanted a man, too, but instead she simply kissed her good-night and slipped out the door. She pressed her back to the wall and took a deep breath.

She wanted a whole family for Megan, but she couldn't tell her the truth—Jeremy didn't want to get involved.

This time, the truth was just too painful.

Chapter Eleven

The next morning, Jeremy was already waiting by her squad car when she made her way outside to go to work. He looked too handsome, wearing a snug pair of jeans that still had the crease of newly bought pants and a fresh plaid shirt that made him look like a logger in all the right ways.

He had a cup of Starbucks coffee in his hand and he extended it to her as she approached. "I hope you accept my peace offering."

She frowned, trying her best to be cute in an

attempt to show him all that he was missing by not choosing her. "What kind is it?"

"Pumpkin spice latte. I even had them put the whipped cream on."

Most of the deputies she worked with loved their coffee unflavored and black—like it was some kind of symbolic gesture that they were tougher than the average person who needed added flavor, cream and sugar in their coffee. Unlike them, she loved pumpkin spice. Did he know, or was it just a lucky guess?

"Whole or skim?"

"Whole milk," he said with that trademark grin he seemed to reserve especially for her. "Nothing but the best for you."

"Thanks." She took the coffee, careful to avoid touching his tanned hands. "Why the sudden about-face?" As she asked the question, she wished she could take it back. That was one conversation she didn't want to open. "Never mind. Don't answer that," she added, trying to put the cork back in the bottle.

"No, you're right. I shouldn't have said what I did."

She waited for "I'm sorry," but it didn't come. Did that mean he shouldn't have said it, but he still meant it?

She took a long drink of the hot coffee, not knowing what to say.

"I was hoping, if you're not upset, I could go with you again today to see the mayor."

So that was it. He wasn't sorry. He was worried about not getting the chance to work on the case. She considered telling him to get lost, but the truth was that she couldn't turn him away when everything centered on his brother... This was personal.

"Fine. Whatever. Get in the car."

He smiled and got in the car, but this time the cute smile didn't have the same stomach-clenching effect. This time she had to withstand the urge to punch him in the nose. Why did all men have to be pains in the behind? Why couldn't they be as simple as they always claimed they were?

She got in and accidentally squealed the tires as she backed out of the driveway. The ride was silent, but she noticed that Jeremy kept glancing over at her as if he was trying to gauge her anger. The third time she noticed him looking her way, she had to bite her tongue to keep from saying something she would regret.

"I talked to Penny this morning, before she went to practice," he said finally, almost like he'd been searching for and found a way to open a conversation that wouldn't bring up anything about last night. "She's playing soccer. Is Megan into sports?"

Did he really think that talking about their kids would make things easier for him?

"Nope."

"Play an instrument?"

"No," she answered, careful to stick to the safe, monosyllabic responses.

"That's too bad," he said, but from the way he peered over at her, it was clear that he wasn't really commenting on Megan's after-school activities, or lack thereof. "Penny loves soccer," he said, looking away, careful to maneuver around her anger. "She's been playing since first grade. She's pretty good, too."

"Oh, yeah?" Blake said as she turned down the main road that led to the mayor's office.

There was a silver Land Rover parked in front of the building. Apparently Engelman was in.

"Look," Jeremy said, pointing to the car as if she hadn't seen it.

"Yep."

He jerked in his seat, as though he'd had enough of her being short with him. "If we're going to go in there together, then we can't be at each other's throats. We need to show him that we're a united front or he's going to take advantage of our weakness."

She wasn't weak, and Jeremy was a fool if he thought she was.

"Then maybe you should stay in the car."

"Stop it, Blake," he said, with a pained expression on his face. "I said I'm sorry."

"No, actually you didn't. Instead you made it abundantly clear that all you care about is the investigation—and that's fine. I get it. Your family is important to you, and—"

I'm not. She stopped before she let the words

fall from her lips. She didn't want to come off as self-pitying.

"You're important to me, too," he said, reaching for her hand, but she pulled it away.

How could he have known what she was thinking?

"That's why I said what I did." He left his hand open between their seats, as if he was waiting for her to place her hand in his. "I don't want either one of us to end up hurt here. We don't live in the same place. We both have lives that, when this is all figured out, are going to pull us in different directions. It would be naive to think we could have it all."

She understood his logic, but her heart screamed for her to be unreasonable—to just pay heed to the way her body wanted him.

"You're right," she said, looking down at his hand. Instead of taking it, she opened her door and got out, closing it so he was out of earshot. "We can't have it all."

THE MAYOR SAT behind his desk, reclining with his feet perched up on the edge like he was midnap. He pulled his feet down as they walked in.

"Deputy West, I heard you might be stopping by," he said, standing up and motioning for them to take a seat. His oversize belly hung low over the waistband of his pants, and his shirt was stretched tight over his paunch. He quickly tried to adjust his suit jacket to cover the stressed buttons.

His office was decorated with a collection of antiquated law books and bronzes of firemen and police officers, replicas and idols of heroes—as if he hoped that some of their traits would rub off on him.

"Thank you for seeing us, Mayor Engelman," she said, sitting down in the proffered chair as Jeremy followed suit. "This is my colleague, Jeremy Lawrence. He's helping our department with an investigation."

"Which investigation would that be?" the mayor asked, flopping down in his seat.

Jeremy leaned forward, resting his elbows on the armrests of the leather chair. "Actually, it's a homicide involving my brother, Robert Lawrence."

The mayor frowned, the action forced and out of place on the practiced features of the politician. "Robert Lawrence," the mayor said, tapping his finger on his lip like he was thinking. "Afraid I haven't heard of him."

"Huh, that's strange," Jeremy said, attacking the mayor's error. "My brother had a picture of you parked at his neighbor's house last week."

"If this guy is your brother, Mr. Lawrence, don't you think that this case is a conflict of interest for you?" the mayor asked, carefully sidestepping Jeremy's accusation.

"My professionalism is not up for debate, Mayor Engelman. However, your association with my brother is."

The mayor laughed. "This isn't some episode of *CSI*. Just because there is a picture of my car near the Whatever It's Called Mine, that doesn't mean I have any kind of association with your brother. What did you say your brother's name was again?"

Jeremy's face darkened, causing Blake to step in and divert what looked to have become a conflagration.

"His brother's name is Robert Lawrence," she said. "We were called out to his place of residence earlier this week. There, we located his remains. I was just hoping we could talk a little bit about it, in the event you could shed some light on the case."

The mayor looked down at his watch as if to say they were wasting his time and he had somewhere better to be. "I appreciate that you're trying to do your job, Deputy West— I do. However, there's nothing I can tell you about your homicide investigation. If all you have is some picture of my car in his neighbor's driveway, I'm not sure why you are standing in my office."

Jeremy's face contorted with rage. "We're standing here because you're a—"

"Vital piece of this investigation," Blake said, once again interrupting just in time to stop Jeremy from saying something that would serve neither of them. She reached down and pulled out the picture of the gun that they had found in the mine next to Robert's body. "Have you seen this gun before?"

The mayor took the photo and studied it. Jeremy looked at her, and she mouthed for him to relax. He jerked his head toward the mayor and mouthed something she couldn't quite make out, but she wasn't sure she needed to as she could still read the contempt that filled Jeremy's eyes. She shook her head, and Jeremy leaned back from the mayor's desk in resignation.

The mayor looked up. "Where did you find this gun?"

"Have you seen it before?" she asked, careful to avoid giving any information. She needed to pull him into the trap, get him to spill the secrets that only the killer would know.

The mayor gave a noncommittal shrug.

It was no wonder the man was a politician.

Here he was, with his feet to the flames, and he looked calm and collected—a far cry from the reaction most people had when they thought they were a suspect in a homicide investigation. For a split second she wondered if that was what the guy was like in bed—noncommittal and dismissive.

She glanced over at Jeremy. His face was red and the vein in his neck was starting to protrude slightly. From their encounter at Robert's cabin, the mere taste of what he was capable of sexually, she had to bet he was the kind of guy who liked to revel in the glory of a woman's body—dipping his fingers down her curves, tracing the lines of her breasts.

What it would have been like to have had the chance to experience all of him…

Her body pulsed with lust. She shifted uncomfortably in her seat, then forced herself to look away and back at the pudgy face of the mayor.

"Yes or no, Mayor? Have you seen this gun before?" she reiterated, pressing her point.

"It's a Glock, isn't it?"

"Is that a 'Yes, I've seen the gun'?"

"It's possible. I just sold a gun like this a few weeks ago."

"You *sold* a gun like this? Or did you buy it?"

The mayor stared at her. "I sold one like it. I can't tell you whether or not it's the same exact gun."

"We were told that you just recently purchased a gun like this. Is that right?"

The mayor's brow furrowed, and he shook his head. "I bought my Glock five years ago from a police auction—your department's, if I recall correctly. I think it was some fundraiser."

He'd had the gun for five years? Things didn't

align. The manager at the range had told them the gun had just been sold to the mayor by Todd O'Brien, but was it possible that the man had gotten it backward?

"Who did you sell the gun to?" Blake asked.

The color leeched from Engelman's face, and his skin took on the color of a dead fish.

"Something wrong, Mayor?" Jeremy asked with a little too much glee in his voice.

"N-no…" the mayor stammered. "I'm fine. I…I think I may know who your brother is after all."

"Is that right," Jeremy said, his voice almost a laugh.

"I sold his neighbor, Todd O'Brien, my gun. My Glock22 Gen 4, like the one here, but I wholeheartedly doubt they're the same weapon."

Blake's excitement bubbled up to the surface

as the mayor scrambled. Finally the pieces were starting to come together.

"Why did you sell him your gun?" Blake asked.

"We both belong to the same gun club, and we got to talking about police-issued firearms. He offered me the right amount of money."

"Do you have a certificate of sale?"

Even though it didn't seem possible, the mayor's color lightened, bordering on translucent. "I…I didn't get one. It was just a spur-of-the-moment thing."

"You, of all people, should know better. Don't you think you should have gotten a receipt, Mayor?" Blake asked.

Some of the man's color returned as his face tightened. He tented his fingers in front of him on the desk. "What are you saying, Deputy West?" His voice carried an air of threat. "Are you saying that you think I had something to do with the murder of Robert Lawrence?"

"We are investigating all possible leads, Mayor." The top button of her collar suddenly felt entirely too tight, and she reached up and undid it.

"If I'm one of your leads, you are fishing in the wrong pool, Deputy." The mayor thumped his hands on the oak desk. "I am an elected official. I am expected to hold myself to a higher standard—and I do. The fact that you would question my credibility and judgment indicates a strong lack of character on your part."

"You're wrong," Jeremy rebuked. "She's doing her job. And her job has led her here. To your office. Maybe it was you who screwed up." Jeremy's face was hard, and his cheeks were red. He looked like he was struggling to keep his emotions in check.

It was strange to watch the normally stoic detective fight so hard. In a way, it made him look even more handsome than he had before, but perhaps it was simply that he was coming to her rescue. As much as she didn't buy into the heroic knight-in-shining-armor fantasy, he was doing a good impression of one.

"The only mistake I've made is letting you in my office," the mayor growled. "You have no grounds to question me."

"Oh, really?" Jeremy continued. "You are connected to the county treasurer, Roger Davy—am I correct?"

"What about him?" The mayor sat back in his chair and crossed his arms over his chest, protecting his core.

"I believe he is your brother-in-law. Yes?"

"So what? I have family. Is this going somewhere, Detective Lawrence? Or are you just grasping at straws in an effort to rid yourself of the guilt of knowing that you are virtually useless in solving your brother's murder?"

Jeremy rose to his feet as the mayor antagonized him.

"Why do you want my brother's property, Engelman?"

"It's Mayor Engelman to you, Detective," he said with a smug grin. "And I don't know what you're talking about. I barely even know who your brother is, let alone anything about his property."

"It's strange that you were photographed near my brother's property and you sold a gun to his neighbor—a neighbor no doubt you knew hated him. Then my brother is slapped with a tax lien. A tax lien that once again points back to you. You know the expression. If it looks like a duck, walks like a duck—"

"I have nothing to do with tax liens." The mayor tensed as some of his polished exterior slipped.

"Then why are you the CEO of one of the largest investment companies that specializes in acquiring tax liens, Mayor Engelman?" Jeremy spat the man's name.

"Get out of my office. Now." The mayor stood up and jabbed his finger toward the door.

Blake stood up, grabbed Jeremy and pulled him to his feet. They didn't need to kick the hornet's nest any more.

"Deputy West, it is my recommendation that you rethink your investigation," Mayor Engelman warned. "And while you are at it, you should start considering alternative job options. You and your superiors may need to think about your long-term career goals."

Chapter Twelve

Once again he'd screwed up. Jeremy leaned against Blake's patrol car, staring at the sidewalk as he waited for Blake to get off the phone. No doubt she was calling her captain and telling him about the mistake he'd made in the mayor's office. Why had he allowed the guy to get under his skin? He was better than that. Yet he had fallen into an emotional pit. Emotions had no role in an investigation—especially not when so much lay on the line. His clouded judgment might not only have affected the investigation, it may also have just cost Blake her job.

She couldn't lose her job. She had her daughter and her mother to support. It was all his fault.

He kicked the curb, sending pain up his foot.

"That's not a soccer ball," Blake said, making her way over to him.

He pushed off the car and limped as he put weight on his foot.

"That hurt?" she asked, walking to the driver's side of the car.

"I'll be fine."

"Well, if it hurts, it serves you right." She opened the door. "I thought you learned your lesson about kicking things in the mayor's office."

"I'm sorry," he said.

She got in the car and slammed the door.

Apparently she didn't want an apology now. It was funny. Earlier she had started a fight to get one, but now that he offered one up on a silver platter, she didn't want it.

He got in before she had the chance to start the car and leave him standing there.

Her face was in shadows, but even somewhat hidden, he could make out her worried expression.

"What did your captain say?" He wasn't sure he wanted to know, but he had to do what he could to stop the catastrophe that could be coming.

"You mean other than he thinks you should go back to Missoula before you start any more political wars?"

"Sure, other than that." He sank down in his seat, one motion away from ducking and covering.

"We have twenty-four hours. Then he thinks the ax is going to fall. Either I have to find the killer or we'll be out on our butts." She turned to face him. "Why did you have to go in there with guns blazing?" She motioned toward the mayor's office. "I had things under control. Instead you just had to confront him, didn't you? Is that how you investigate things—by starting a fight?"

"I'm a good detective, Blake." He felt weak saying it, but it was all he could think of in his defense. "I screwed up. We both know I screwed up. But there's no going back. From now on I'll do everything I can to make this right." *Even if it means costing me everything.*

"I'm not sure what we can do, other than find the killer. Even then, it doesn't mean that I will have this job by week's end."

"Engelman can't just fire you. There has to be a reason, besides pissing off the wrong people."

Blake laughed. "Have you been living in a hole your entire life? Sure, he can't put the real grievance on file, but if he can't find something that he can fire me for, he'll make my life miserable until he gets what he needs. He'll get his way. He always does. That's why he's the mayor."

Jeremy wanted to pull her into his arms and tell her everything would be okay. That he would fix everything. Yet he couldn't. Not after what had happened. They'd both made themselves clear on where they stood—and how each of them didn't have time or a place in their lives for a relationship. If he took her in his embrace, he wasn't sure that he could stop himself from all the feelings that seemed to flood through him when she was near. He couldn't risk losing his heart to love, especially to a woman who, right now, probably hated him—and had every right.

He thought about what Blake said. How the only way out was to solve the case. They had twenty-four hours. And he knew what they had to do. "Let's start at Todd O'Brien's. If what the mayor said was at all true, he's the man we need to see."

"He was the next one on my list."

He wasn't sure if her annoyed tone was because he had told her what he thought they should do, or if it was because he'd made another misstep in their investigation. Whatever was behind it, he had to fix it. "Did you get any results on the ballistics?"

She nodded. "They ran tests yesterday. The bullet that killed Robert was definitely from that gun, but they didn't get much on the fingerprints."

"What do you mean?"

"They found a single print from an index finger, but it wasn't one they had in the database. The only thing the tech said is that, based on the way they held the gun, the person was left-handed and they had some kind of scar on their index finger."

They could use that. "Did they pull any kind of serial number from the gun?"

"The ballistic expert tried to do an X-ray diffraction, but whoever took out the number had stippled the metal, effectively removing any trace."

There were not a lot of people who knew how or what kind of tools could create such a degree of precision in removing numbers.

He thought about the gun. A police-issued

firearm. He had a feeling it was chosen especially for this murder.

Whoever did this was laughing at them.

"We need to be careful."

"Huh?" Blake asked.

"The person behind this doesn't have respect
for law enforcement. They think they're above
the law. They've killed once, and they won't
hesitate to do it again. If we get close, our lives
might be in danger."

Blake shook her head. "Just because we made
a mistake in there," she said, pointing to the
office, "doesn't mean that you have to be dramatic. We're fine."

Her words made goose bumps rise on his
arms. Anytime he'd ever gotten complacent in
his job, or thought he was safe, was when he'd
found himself in trouble.

"Think about it, Blake." Her name felt like

velvet on his tongue; it even tasted sweet. He paused as he just looked at her for a moment.

"What?" she asked, locking eyes with him.

"Who do you know who hates law enforcement and we've been circling?"

"Todd O'Brien."

"Exactly. If we go out there, you need to be careful. Who knows what he'll do?"

"That's crazy. I've dealt with him plenty of times. He's all bark and no bite." She shook her head.

"You're right. But this time when we go out there, it'll be different. This time he's the suspect in a murder investigation."

"He won't know that."

"If he has anything to do with Robert's death, he will. Don't underestimate this guy. We have reports that he has an active shooting range. This guy is skilled with firearms. He has had run-ins with law enforcement, and you, before. O'Brien seems to fit the bill of our suspect. He's has a need and certainly had the opportunity to kill Robert."

Blake gripped the steering wheel until her knuckles turned white.

Todd O'Brien's property looked more like a hoarder's hovel than the homestead of someone who was bragging that he was soon going to be a millionaire. The driveway was long and winding. As they drove farther and farther into the darkening forest, a pit grew in Blake's stomach. She reached down and checked her phone. The bars flicked from three to none every few feet. Hopefully they wouldn't need to call in assistance.

Her bulletproof vest pressed against her breasts, chafing her underarms as the car bounced on the cobbles and ruts that littered the road. Todd O'Brien was a miserable, angry person and likely had something to do with Robert's death, but she didn't think he would try to gun her down. They'd known each other for years. Though, admittedly, things had been growing tenser between them ever since trouble had started to brew between him and Robert.

She had never thought it would end like this—her investigating him for murder while being stuck in the car with her high school crush, who, once again, was completely unavailable.

Todd's house sat at the end of the long drive and was surrounded by overgrown brush. The weeds listed to the left like even they didn't want to be associated with the place. As Blake and Jeremy approached the front door, they were greeted by the bay of a hound dog and a rattle, as it must have jumped against the chain-link fence of its kennel in the back.

The entire place smelled like rotting vegetation and compost. In the distance, there was a small garden complete with a one-armed scarecrow that had almost completely fallen from his post. The stuffed creature looked like a drunken man, one arm sprawled over the edge of the wood, holding himself up from falling into the dirty reality that waited. Sitting on the post, above the scarecrow's head, was a large raven. It watched them, its black eye catching the little rays of sun that filtered through the forest.

Though she'd been here before, this time the place gave her the heebie-jeebies. She tried to shake off the feeling.

Jeremy walked beside her, looking confident yet cautious as he strode up the steps and knocked on Todd's door.

"Hello? Anyone home?" Blake called.

The lights were on in the living room, and she could just make out the back of Todd's balding head.

He turned and looked at them, then slowly got up from the couch and made his way to the door. The hair around his ears had grown so long that it had started to ducktail and made the bald spot on the top even more pronounced. "What are you doing here?"

"Sorry to bother you, Mr. O'Brien," she said, completely out of habit and training rather than out of genuine emotions.

Todd grumbled something unintelligible. As he moved, his face caught a shadow that filled the craters under his eyes. He mustn't have been sleeping lately, or else he had been drinking heavily.

She stepped closer. The man smelled like last night's booze and a week without a shower. That was unlike Todd. Every time she had been there in the last few years, he had been the picture of a man who had himself together. Why the sudden shift in demeanor?

"How's it going, Todd?" she asked, trying to lower his guard.

"What do you care?"

Jeremy leaned against the door frame and slid his foot into the house far enough that Todd couldn't slam the door in their faces.

"Ah, come on, Todd," he said. "Let's not be like that."

"Why are you here?"

"I was just hoping to ask you a few questions about Robert," Blake answered.

He nodded. "I figured you would be up here. It was only a matter of time. But I'm telling you, I ain't got nothing to do with his death."

"I'm glad to hear you say that," she said, but she wasn't really sure if she meant it or not. It would be so easy if this was their man. Everything could be solved, the mayor would be appeased and Jeremy would go home. Everything would go back to the way it was. Then again, she could never live with herself if she pinned the murder on an innocent man. "I know you had your fair share of problems with Robert Lawrence."

"You're right, but that don't mean I'm stupid enough to get mixed up in somebody killing him."

Jeremy tensed. "How do you know someone killed him? We haven't released that information to the press."

Todd scowled, revealing a large crooked scar along the side of his temple. "It don't take no rocket scientist to see what's going on here. Don't you be trying to put words in my mouth. I told you. I ain't got nothing to do with his death."

"Then how did you know it was a murder, Todd?" Blake pressed.

Todd looked at her. "You know as well as I do, West. This is a small town. Word spreads faster than weeds."

"Then do you want to tell us about the gun?" Jeremy asked, taking the lead in the questioning.

"What gun?"

"The gun you bought from the mayor. The same caliber gun that was used to kill my brother."

Todd stepped back from the door until his

body rested against the back of a chair. He reminded her of the scarecrow in the garden, one strong breeze away from being thrust into the dirt.

"You're right. I bought a gun from Engelman, but it got stolen."

"Is that right?" Blake asked, stepping in front of Jeremy to preempt his questions. "Did you report it stolen?"

"I only figured it out yesterday."

Jeremy smirked as things fell apart for Todd.

"I swear I didn't have nothing to do with Robert's death. We didn't like each other, but I didn't want to kill him."

"If you don't tell us what you know, O'Brien, we're more than happy to take you in," Jeremy said, his tone low and threatening. "I'm sure forty-eight hours in the interrogation room will help you come clean."

"Wait," Todd said, raising his hands. "I'm tellin' you the truth. That gun was stolen about a week ago. I'd taken it out when—" Todd stopped and looked at them as if he hoped they hadn't heard what he'd said. "Wait…I get it. Someone who wanted me to take the fall."

"When did you take out the gun, Todd?" Jeremy pressed.

"I dunno, but that thing was taken."

"The DA is going to have a field day with you in court. You're looking at a life sentence with a defense like that."

The blood drained from Todd's sun-crisped face.

"I didn't do nothing. I'm a taxpayer. You work for me. How dare you come in my house and start threatening me?"

"We're not threatening you, Todd." Blake

watched Todd's exterior crack and all his insecurities come tumbling out.

"That's BS. You came out here with the intention of intimidating me. You have no right. You have nothing. I didn't have nothing to do with Robert's death, and I ain't seen his dumb wife."

They hadn't mentioned a single word about Tiffany. Jeremy looked to her and raised his eyebrows. He had heard Todd's slip, as well.

They were standing on the wolf's tail. If they weren't careful, he would attack, but they couldn't decrease the pressure. They needed to make him lose his edge. To tell them everything he knew. Everything he was attempting to hide.

Chapter Thirteen

It was late in the afternoon, and they were still waiting. With any luck the judge would issue the search warrant in time for them to get back to Todd's place before it got dark. If not, they would have to wait until the morning when they could get enough manpower to serve the papers and pick the place apart.

"How's your burger?" Jeremy asked as Blake took a bite of the bar fare.

She shrugged. "Fine," she said, pointing at his untouched basket of food. "You gonna eat that?"

It was the reality of being a law enforcement officer that when he was given the chance to eat, he needed to take it. This job could keep him on the streets well into the night.

"I'm not hungry," he said, pushing a fry around the basket.

She snorted as she swallowed a bite. "These burgers are the best in town. You're missing out." She dabbed at her mouth with a napkin.

He glanced at her phone, hoping at any moment it would ding with the message they'd gotten their search warrant.

"Look, it's like a pot," she said, motioning toward her phone. "It's not going to boil if you're constantly watching it."

She was right, but he couldn't help himself. He hated the fact that they had to leave O'Brien's compound. Todd knew something about Robert's death, and leaving him standing there, when they were so close to some-one with answers, was torturous. Yet there'd been little they could do, or find, without a warrant. Once they got it, they would be back. Then they would hopefully get everything they needed to pin this guy down.

"Did you get a chance to look over Robert and Tiffany's credit card reports?" he asked, still staring at the phone. "Anything that could help us get a lead on Tiffany's whereabouts?"

"I forwarded you a copy of the email from Wells Fargo." Blake had a pained expression.

What wasn't she saying?

He opened up the email on his phone and went through the list of recent purchases: min-ing supplies, Walmart, Home Depot...normal shopping. Nothing that stood out. The only thing irregular over the last six months of his brother's and sister-in-law's purchases was the fact that both of them had stopped using their credit cards the day of Robert's death.

"There's also an email about bank records." Blake took another bite, avoiding his gaze.

Jeremy opened the second email and clicked through their banking records. Just like their credit card there were the normal bills: electric, garbage and mortgage. He scrolled down to deposits and withdrawals. According to the records, there had been an $18,250 cash withdrawal a week before Robert went missing. The bank's statement didn't indicate who had pulled out the money.

He set his phone down on the brown Formica table, but he couldn't look away from the bank statement. There was the withdrawal request and the card used, but it didn't tell him who exactly took out the money. The longer he looked at the withdrawal, the more it seemed to pulse with life, as if the number itself was trying to tell him something.

"We need to get to the bank. See if we can get their surveillance videos and see whether it was Robert or Tiffany who pulled out the money," he said, pushing up from his seat.

"Sit down and eat," Blake said, motioning toward his food. "There's nothing we can do until tomorrow. The banks are closed."

She was right, but it didn't stop his blood pressure from creeping higher. He waved toward the bartender as he settled back into the hard wooden chair. "Can I get a Bud Light, bottle?"

He knew he shouldn't drink when they were working on an investigation, but he needed something to take the edge off. He just needed a moment, a second, to stop and think.

The bartender sat a bottle on a tiny napkin in front of him.

"Thanks," he said, taking a long drink. The bitter taste flooded his senses. He was more of a scotch man, but the beer would do.

A man who was sitting at the bar kept glancing over at them as Jeremy started to eat his burger. When they entered any public place it was as if every eye was on them and everyone wanted to hear what they were talking about.

He looked to Blake, but she didn't seem to notice the attention they were drawing—she seemed hyperfocused on the burger in her hands.

"What are you thinking?" he asked, taking another drink and trying to ignore the man at the bar.

Blake took a long sip of her Coke, like she

was avoiding having to answer him, but he waited her out.

"About Tiffany and what Todd said..." she started, but then stopped, as if she was unsure of what exactly to say.

"What about them?"

She remained silent as she spun the red plastic straw around in her pop.

"You think she's dead, don't you?" He tapped on the phone, calling her attention to the financial transactions that had suddenly stopped.

Blake looked up at him, her blue eyes were full of questions. "What do you think? You think it's possible?"

He had been a detective for too many years to be naive. There was a good chance his sister-in-law was dead. Then again, it was more than a little fishy that someone would pull out all their money, and then they find one body but not the other. For all he knew, maybe Tiffany was the one behind Robert's murder. Maybe she took the money, Robert found out and she killed him. Whoever had shot his brother had to be someone who could get close, close enough that he wouldn't stop the killer when he or she came at him with a gun.

Then again, a Glock .40 caliber had one hell of a kick. Tiffany was a small woman. If she was trying to shoot Robert, could she have done it in a single shot with such precision?

Normally, in the case of a shooting death, there was more than one shot if there was any form of altercation. The first shot would be low, near the floor as the person tried to fend off the attack. Then there was some kind of kill shot. In the cases of homicide that he usually saw, the second and third shots were to the chest. But not in Robert's case. One shot to the head. Execution-style. There was no low shot. No evidence of defensive wounds. Nothing to indicate anything other than his brother had sat there and taken a shot to the head.

It wasn't like Robert.

His thoughts drifted to his brother's letter. *The thing I love most would be the death of me.*

Had that been Robert's final clue that his wife had been behind his death? He had hidden the note in his waistband. He must have been afraid someone would find it…someone besides law enforcement…someone who would pat down his body when he died. Who would have been capable of doing that, and why?

Maybe whoever was after him wanted his money. Maybe it was Tiffany. Maybe she wanted to take him for every last penny before she disappeared. It was possible she'd started a fight with him in the mine, shot and killed him, then imploded the entrance, thinking that he would never be found.

Yet if she was behind the murder, why hadn't she just stayed put? She could have told anyone that Robert had simply run off, gone to Mexico. His parents would have been upset. No doubt Jeremy would have looked into the disappearance, but if she had taken the time, she could have covered up any foul play long before he arrived. It would have taken some time and some planning, but it wasn't out of the question.

She could have walked away with everything. The money, the house, the mine.

She had to be dead.

If she was dead, Todd O'Brien seemed like the most logical suspect. Why else would Todd have brought her up? Why had he acted so guilty when it came to her?

The guy hated Robert. Maybe he was trying to take everything of Robert's in one fell swoop.

Normally Jeremy loved a good mystery, but not this time…not when the deceased was his brother.

He was about to ask Blake what she thought, but he stopped as the man at the bar stood up and started to walk toward them. The guy walked with a limp, like he had a problem with his hip. As he moved, Jeremy noticed the familiar line of a holstered gun concealed under the man's blue flannel shirt.

His hand tightened on the sweaty beer bottle. It seemed everyone in Montana had a gun and many had a concealed weapon permit, but it always made him twitch. There was no way of knowing what a person was capable of.

"Sorry for bothering y'all," the man said with

a congenial smile. "I heard about your case out at the Foreman Mine."

"Does everyone know what happened out there?" he asked Blake, who sent him a knowing smile that reminded him exactly how small the town was.

"I live just in the ravine over from the mine," the man continued. "A few weeks back, Robert and Todd had guns out and I had to call you guys. Thought things were gonna take an ugly turn, if you know what I mean."

Jeremy's grip loosened on his beer bottle. "Is that right?"

The man nodded. "Yep, but normally I ain't got no problem with Todd. He's got land on the other side of mine. Comes through every few days to check it out, walk the fence line and make sure everything is as it should be."

"He has land on the *other* side of yours? What do you mean?" Blake asked.

"He's been buying up land left and right out near me. Been lots of foreclosures after the downturn in the economy and the uptick in taxes. Everyone's been havin' problems making ends meet. Some even been selling to him before the bank takes over."

His thoughts instantly moved to Robert. Had he been one of the ones Todd had been buying out?

Blake's phone chimed to life. She picked it up and then looked to him. "We have our warrant," she whispered after a moment.

She looked beautiful as her features lit with exuberance. Obviously she loved this chase, this bringing the wicked to their knees, as much as he did. As he watched her, he couldn't help the feeling of desire that rose in him. She wanted justice, and he wanted her that much more for it.

"You're a smart one, friend," Blake said turning back to the man at their table. "How many properties, that you know of, does Todd own?"

"The name's Court," he said. "And I dunno about how many properties Todd's bought, but I bet he's got at least a couple hundred acres of land."

"And you said he has access to some through your property?"

"He pays me an easement fee. He wouldn't have to if Robert had sold to him, but it works out great for me. It's like free money coming in every month." Court moved to sit down, carefully adjusting his hip and leg as he lowered his body.

"What do you do?" Jeremy asked.

"Now?" Court asked. "Now I'm retired, but

before they downsized, I used to work for the mine adjacent to the Berkeley Pit. I fed the crusher. Malachite, pyrite and matrix on the front end, crushed ore on the other," the man said with an air of nostalgia. "I walked away with a decent retirement when the mine closed, but it didn't cover everything. Unfortunately, I had to sell off quite a bit of my land. That's how Todd got his hands on the land on the other side of my parcel. It's why I had to give him an easement."

Everything was coming back to Todd. They just needed to find the link that brought it all together and proved, without a doubt, that Todd had murdered Robert.

"At least I had it easy, and he was willing to pay me," Court continued.

"What do you mean?" Jeremy asked, trying to follow Court's train of thought.

"Your brother, he didn't want nothing to do with Todd. He hated him—along with the rest of us. From what I heard, Todd wanted to buy out your brother's place, but your brother wasn't interested. Todd was real pushy about it, something about how it was important to his investors."

And there it was. They had their motive. All they needed was probable cause, and they could bring down Robert's killer.

Chapter Fourteen

Two deputies followed them down the dirt road. They pulled to a stop well away from where Todd could see them from anywhere on his main property.

Jeremy looked positively antsy as he tapped his fingers on the base of the window. Sometimes he surprised her; for a detective, the man had a lot of tells.

Blake wasn't sure if it was because he had a young daughter or if it was something else that made him seem so different from all the other men in her life, but whatever it was it didn't help the way he made her feel. It would have been so much easier to push him away if he was the emotionless creature that most detectives seemed to be. Instead there he was, smiling while he looked out the window as the late afternoon glistened off his short dark hair.

Damn him for looking like a Hollywood star midpose.

She forced herself to look away as one of the deputies approached her window. No one else could think there was any type of relationship forming between them. They were nothing but friends, close, old-time friends. The kiss they'd shared could be nothing but a fading memory, an impulsive whim—no matter how badly she wanted to feel his lips again.

"Deputy West, we'll go in and take control over O'Brien while you execute the warrant. Sound good?" the deputy asked.

She glanced over to Jeremy. "That's fine," she said. "Just make sure you're ready. O'Brien may or may not have killed a man. Don't get on the wrong side of him."

The deputy nodded and returned to his car. They crept up the road and to Todd's driveway.

"You need to be careful," Jeremy said, finally looking at her. "He has to know we're coming. And if he does, he's going to be ready. This guy thinks he's above the law."

"Are you worried about me, Jeremy?" she asked, sounding impish as she tried to put him on the spot about how he felt about her.

He looked at her as if he was the one searching for answers, but she tried to keep her emotions in check.

He opened his mouth to speak, but she cut him off. "Never mind," Blake said, suddenly regretting the attempt to make him tell her what he felt. "I'll be careful in there. But you need to be focused on what you need to do. Keep yourself safe."

He closed his mouth and looked away. Instead of relief, regret filled her. She should never have hinted at her feelings. She was being ridiculous, setting herself up to take another fall. Men, she could handle. The only truly dangerous things were feelings.

They pulled to a stop in front of Todd's house, next to one of the cars that had been covered by a tarp. She stepped beside the concealed vehicle and, out of curiosity, lifted the tarp. Underneath was a maroon late 1990s model Buick. "You see this?" she asked Jeremy as she motioned to the car.

"What about it?"

"It look familiar to you?"

Jeremy shook his head, and she dropped

the tarp back into place. Whatever they were looking for was inside Todd's house. His lights were on inside, illuminating the shadows that had started to fall over the place as dusk crept through the landscape.

She strode up to the porch, her hand on her Glock. Her heart hammered in her chest, but she tried to tell herself it was nothing more than Jeremy and his warning. This was nothing, just another search warrant being served. They would get the evidence they needed to tie Todd to the crime, arrest him and be back to normal before midnight. Heck, if things went really well, she could be home in time to tuck Megan into bed.

Thinking of Megan only made her heart beat louder in her ears.

She couldn't lose her edge. She couldn't let her fear beat her.

She took out her flashlight and tapped the heavy aluminum impromptu billy club against the door. "Sheriff's department!" she yelled. "Todd, answer the door!"

She stepped back, readying herself to kick, but just as her weight shifted to her left foot and she started to raise the right, Todd appeared in the large rectangular window of the door.

"What do you want? I told you I didn't do nothing!" he yelled through the window.

She pressed the search warrant against the glass, right in his face. "You can open the door or we can kick it down. Either way, we are coming in and searching your property!"

Todd stepped back, turning his back to them. Then she heard a slide and a click, the metallic sound of a round being racked into the chamber of a gun. She drew her gun and lifted it, pointing at Todd's center of mass.

"Don't do anything stupid, Todd. Just open the door and come out with your hands up!"

"I didn't kill Robert. I didn't do nothing wrong. Why can't you just leave me the hell alone?" Todd yelled.

"If you didn't do anything, then just let us in. Let us complete our investigation. If you're innocent, you have nothing to worry about. Don't create more problems by making bad decisions. Put down the gun and open the door!"

Todd was silent, and she let the seconds tick by, hoping that he would make the choice that would keep the situation from escalating. The last thing she wanted to do was get in a shootout and have to call down the full SWAT team. Everyone in the state would hear about the incident by the end of the day. The higher-ups would be pissed at the level of scrutiny they would have to go through. And she'd have to face the consequences.

Jeremy lowered to his knee on the other side of the door, taking a lower charge position. "Listen to Blake. Come out with your hands up, Todd."

"I wasn't even here the day your brother died. I swear," Todd argued. "I'd gone to Missoula for the day."

Jeremy sent her a questioning glance. Was such a thing possible?

"That's great, Todd. That's what we need to know. Is there anyone who can testify to your whereabouts?" Blake asked.

They were met with another long silence. If Todd was smart, he was thinking about the consequences that would befall him if he continued to play such a dangerous game. Yet she doubted he was that smart. More than likely he was thinking about a way to cut and run.

"I drove to Missoula, went to Costco and came back."

"What time did you leave?" Blake asked.

"I don't know. I don't keep a journal!" Todd spat.

His insolence didn't help his case.

"Come out, Todd. Let's talk about this like adults. Let's get this straightened out. There's no need for you to get into more trouble," Blake said.

In truth, the moment he exited that house he'd be down on the ground and arrested for felony assault on a police officer, but at least he'd come out alive.

"You've always been gunning for me, West," Todd said. "I ain't never done nothin' but pay my taxes and try to make a damned living in this forsaken town. What's so wrong with that?"

"There's nothing wrong with that, Todd. But there is something wrong when your neighbor turns up dead and you won't tell us what you know. Come on, now—make the right choice. This is your last chance. If you come out now, we don't have to get ugly. Put down your gun. Step outside."

Todd stepped from the door, and she watched through the window as he made his way to the center of the room. Then he looked at her and smiled. It was the grin of the crazed, cheeks high, a wild glaze in the eyes.

"I never wanted things to go like this," he said as he raised his gun.

The sound of the gunshot ripped through the air, the cacophony roaring in Blake's ears.

"Get down!" Jeremy yelled, reaching over and pulling at her bulletproof vest.

Todd fired again. Blake dropped to the ground. Her face pressed against the cold, jagged wood of the porch. It ripped at her skin, but all she could focus on was the *thump, thump, thump* of her heart and the burning heat rising from her chest.

She looked up. There were two holes in the wall to the side of the door—right where she had been standing.

Jeremy covered her body with his, protecting her from the gunfire. The weight of his body comforted her and made her feel safe. Jeremy wanted to protect her, to keep her away from the evils of the world. He may have said he didn't care about her, that what they felt wasn't real, but his actions said otherwise.

The heat in her chest intensified, stealing her

breath. She reached down and touched the spot right near her armpit. Warm, sticky wetness coated her fingertips. Raising her fingers, she saw blood.

A third shot cut through the air. There was a thump as something hit the floor.

"I'm fine," she said, wiping her fingers off on the boards of the porch. "It's okay. I'm fine," she repeated in an effort to calm herself.

"Suspect is down!" the officer from behind them yelled.

There was the crackle of radios and hurried orders. She could hear the dispatcher talking as she spread the news of the shoot-out radio-wide.

Everyone would know. Everyone would judge her. And soon everyone would know she'd failed at keeping herself and her unit safe.

Jeremy stood up, weapon ready. The backup

officer stepped around him and kicked in the door, sending splinters of wood and glass raining down. She moved to stand up, but the pain in her chest kept her pinned to the ground.

"He's down," Jeremy said, glancing back at her.

His mouth opened in horror.

"Blake…" he said with a long, shocked exhale.

She tried to stand up again, just to prove to him that she was okay, but as she pushed herself up, her arm collapsed beneath her.

Two shots. Two hits.

Jeremy dropped to his knees beside her and rolled her over. "We have an officer down! Officer down!" he screamed, panic searing his voice.

She closed her eyes as the pain racked her body. Her chest was tight, and she struggled to breathe. The world shrank as her body went into shock and her vision tunneled.

"You're going to be okay." Jeremy reached down and ran his hand over her hair, comforting her. "Everything's going to be okay. EMTs are on their way."

"Don't go," she pleaded.

"I'm not going anywhere. As long as you need me, I'll be at your side," Jeremy said, taking her hand and giving it a gentle squeeze.

She stared into his eyes. At their centers was a veil of fear. She wrapped her fingers around his. "And I'll be at yours."

He leaned down, surprising her as he kissed her lips. Some of the pain she was feeling slipped away, replaced with the warmth she felt in his kiss—a kiss that she'd keep in her heart regardless of what life, or death, would bring.

"Suspect is down, but breathing!" the deputy

in the house yelled. "Looks like he tried to off himself!"

Jeremy leaned back and looked inside. "I'll keep you safe. He won't be able to hurt you again."

Numbness started to fill her, moving from the bullet wound in the side of her chest and spreading through her body. Her thoughts went to her daughter. She had to make it out of this alive. Leaving her daughter wasn't an option.

"Megan..." Blake said, struggling to catch her breath as darkness shrouded her vision. "Tell Megan that I'll be okay. Tell her I'll be coming home."

And then all she saw was blackness.

Chapter Fifteen

Hell was sitting in a hospital waiting room. The quiet of the late night only made the agony he felt that much more palpable. No amount of magazines and monotonous television could keep Jeremy calm—not when Blake was through the doors that led to the OR. He clenched his fists as he stared at the entrance to the surgery area. No doubt the hospital staff would stop him if he rushed through those stupid doors.

He took a drink from the bitter, stale coffee that seemed to be ever present in hospitals. He prayed someone would come out and tell him what was happening. He needed to know that she was okay. That she was alive. That she would make it through this.

His whole life he had spent trying to protect his mother and father, their marriage, his brothers—constantly trying to fix the problems they created for themselves. He'd tried his damnedest to save his marriage. But no matter where he went, it seemed like he always screwed it up. His parents were fighting now more than ever, his marriage was over, his brother was dead, his sister-in-law was missing and the woman he cared about was fighting for her life.

Everything he struggled to keep safe had ended in disaster. To solve a problem you needed to calculate the common denominator—in this case, it was him and the curse he seemed to bring onto those nearest him. The best thing he could do for those he loved was to stay out of the equation. He could love from a distance.

All the proof he needed to prove his theory could be found in his daughter, Penny. He hadn't seen her in three weeks. She was the only thing going right in his world…and he barely saw her. She was safe.

Gemma West slammed the door as she barged into the waiting room, Megan at her side. She looked around until she spotted him and then charged over to where he sat. "What in God's name happened, Jeremy?"

The guilt he'd been feeling multiplied, filling every part of his soul. "I'm sorry, Mrs. West." He couldn't bear looking into her eyes and dropped his head into his hands in shame. "I'm so sorry. I tried to keep her safe."

Mrs. West placed her hand on his shoulder,

easing some of his self-hatred. "Jeremy, I have no doubt. I know how much you love her."

He jerked, looking up at her as he started to argue, but he stopped as he caught her gaze. Mrs. W gave him a soft, knowing smile.

Was she right? Did he love Blake? He couldn't argue that he felt...something.

He had never forgotten the first time he realized that he thought of her as more than a friend. She must have been about fifteen. If he closed his eyes he knew he could see her, standing out in the sunshine, her blond hair catching the rays and shining like pure gold. She had looked so happy, the light dancing through her hair and warmth radiating through her body. They'd both been so young. It wasn't long after that she'd gotten pregnant and fallen in love with another man. It had been his first, but hardly his last, lesson in rejection.

Could the pain of that rejection finally heal? Could he love her again? It didn't seem possible when you hurt that much that the whisper of love could make it all disappear.

No matter what he felt, life still stood in the way.

The door to the OR opened, and a doctor walked into the waiting room. The man looked around until he caught sight of them and then made his way over. "Are you the family of Blake West?"

Jeremy looked over at Mrs. West, who gave him a slight nod of the head.

"We are," Jeremy said. "How's she doing? Did she make it?"

The man had the dark circles under his eyes that most nightshift workers seemed to have. Jeremy looked down at his hands. His wrists were red where his latex gloves must have pressed into his skin during the surgery.

"Things are looking good. She took a round to the chest and one to the upper arm. She was extremely lucky that neither bullet hit a major blood vessel. The bullet that hit her arm only missed her brachial artery by a matter of millimeters. If it had been two millimeters to the right, she would have likely bled out on-scene." For the first time, the doctor looked down and seemed to notice Megan standing there. "I'm sorry," he said, motioning toward her. "Would you rather we talked about this somewhere else?"

Mrs. W turned to Megan. "Meg, would you please run and get us each a Coke? There's a pop machine just down the hall." She slipped her some money, and the girl edged her way toward the machine.

She looked back, her face drawn, as she made it to the door. "But, Grandma…" Megan started.

"Run along, honey. Don't worry. I'll fill you in as soon as we know what's going on. I promise."

Megan stayed glued to the spot for a moment longer, but she finally turned away.

The doctor hesitated until the waiting room door closed, and then he continued. "We removed the bullet from her chest. It was lodged in her rib, and we were afraid that, left untreated, it would cause her problems down the road."

"She was wearing a bulletproof vest," Jeremy argued.

The doctor nodded. "The bullet hit her just to the side of her vest. In fact, you'll have to take a look, but it actually nicked the Kevlar, which slowed it down and sent it off course. If she hadn't been wearing the vest, things could have been much, much worse."

"The bullet didn't hit her lung?" Jeremy asked, relief filling him.

"Thankfully it didn't enter the chest cavity," the doctor said. "She was extremely lucky that whoever did this was using a small-caliber weapon. Anything larger and she would have likely suffered significantly more catastrophic wounds."

"What is her prognosis, Doctor?" Mrs. W asked, holding on to the back of one of the blue vinyl chairs that were scattered throughout the room.

"She'll stay in the hospital overnight, but she should be going home in the morning. She will need to take it easy for the next few days and stick to her pain meds and antibiotics. If she does, she shouldn't have any residual problems. Though, again, she'll have to take care of herself."

If there was one thing Blake wasn't good at, it was standing still. This recovery would be hard on her—especially given the circumstances of their investigation.

"Mrs. West," Jeremy said, turning toward her. "Would you mind checking on Megan? I need to ask the doctor here a few more questions."

Mrs. W's face was unmoving, and Jeremy had a hard time reading her.

"Are you going to be okay, Mrs. W?" he asked, noting her pale cheeks.

"Fine, just fine," she said, forcing a smile. "Please take care of my little girl, Doctor."

The doctor answered with a nod, and she made her way from the room.

Jeremy watched as Mrs. W walked past the windows that looked out into the hallway. He turned to the doctor. "So about Todd O'Brien, did you treat him, as well?"

The doctor looked back toward the OR, as if he would rather be in the hot zone of the surgery center instead of standing in the icy chill of a detective's stare.

"Doctor?" Jeremy pushed for an answer. "Did O'Brien survive?"

The doctor wrung his hands and sat down on the chair next to him. He rubbed his hands over his face like he was tired. "I evaluated Mr. O'Brien."

"And?"

"The bullet penetrated the skull and, from the CT scans, it appears to be lodged in his frontal lobe."

"But he's alive. Will he make it?"

"He sustained a great deal of damage to his brain, so he may not. However, if there's an area of the brain that can handle an injury like this, it's the frontal lobe. It's an incredible area, Detective. Some people who have injuries to this area have little to no effects in their daily life, however others…" He trailed off.

"Others, what?"

"Maybe it's better if you talk to the neurologist handling his case."

"No. I want answers now," Jeremy urged. "What could happen to him?"

The doctor tapped his fingers together. "From where he placed the gun on his temple and the location of the lesion, he sustained the most damage to his right frontal area. Sometimes this can change a person's social behavior. They will talk excessively, have less facial control and few facial movements as they speak."

"Do you think his memory will be altered?"

The doctor gave a noncommittal shrug. "The frontal lobe controls the working memory. Damage can affect people in a variety of ways, so *if* he regains consciousness and begins speaking, it's hard to say how he'll respond. Some of these patients lose portions of their short-term and long-term memory, but others…well, there's no effect at all."

So Todd O'Brien might never give him a statement.

A traumatic brain injury that impaired cognitive function could be Todd's golden ticket. Undoubtedly, as soon as he was released from the hospital he would be tried as a felon in the shooting and likely found guilty. However, with the little information they had, and no admission of guilt, it would be hard to prove his role, if any, in Robert's death. But Jeremy had to try. He had to find more evidence. Something that proved, without a doubt, that Todd was guilty.

Or innocent.

He stopped for a second and just stared at the white fake marble squares on the floor. Could Todd be innocent? There was a tiny flicker in his core that told him it was possible. Yet if he was innocent, why had he acted out and shot Blake? He had to be guilty. No innocent man acted like Todd. He was guilty of something, something he was afraid of going to jail for, but whether or not he had pulled the trigger in Robert's death was up for debate.

He stood up. "Thanks, Doc."

"Absolutely," the doctor said, relief filling his voice. "If you have any more questions, please don't hesitate to contact me or the neurologist handling Mr. O'Brien's case."

"Can I see Blake now?"

The doctor nodded. "I had my team move her to the Med-Surg floor. She's still pretty heavily sedated, but she's awake. If you like, you and your family are welcome to go visit her."

He walked out with the doctor, making sure to thank him as they parted ways. Mrs. W and Megan were standing by the pop machine, each holding a can as he approached.

"Everything okay?" Mrs. West asked.

He wasn't sure how to answer. The key suspect in their murder investigation was now an unreliable witness. Even if he confessed, Jeremy wasn't sure that they could actually use his testimony in court.

As much as he hated to admit it, he wished that Todd would have died…that his self-inflicted gunshot wound would have done the trick. In this line of work, he wasn't supposed to feel anything. Everything was supposed to be observed and held at arm's length in order to save his sanity. Yet he couldn't. Not on this case. He was too close.

This case was going to destroy him.

"The doctor said we could see Blake now." He looked at Megan and took the girl's hands in his own. "Meg, your mom's hurt. You heard what the doctor said, right?"

Her blond hair hung limply in her face as she nodded. "I know."

He gave her hands a reassuring squeeze. "Don't worry. Your mom's going to be all right. She's coming home tomorrow."

Megan looked up at him and into his eyes. "Really?"

"Yeah, but here's the deal..." He smiled. "I need you to help her, okay? No more messing with her handcuffs, okay? Can you do that… just for me?"

She pushed her hair out of her face and nodded. "I'll be good. I promise. I'll even make her food and stuff. She loves potato soup."

"Is that right?" Jeremy said, putting his arm around Megan. "I think that would be a great idea."

Megan hugged his arm into her chest. "I wish you were always here."

He smiled.

Mrs. W looked at him with a shimmer in her eyes as his heart moved with joy and an edge of sadness. He missed Penny. He missed these moments with his daughter. He looked at Megan. She looked so much like her…they could almost be sisters. Penny was close to the same age; they had the same blond hair and the same smatter of freckles over their noses.

Against his better judgment his thoughts moved to the future. Megan and Blake could be his life—if only he followed his heart. Penny would approve. She'd always wanted a sibling.

It was a beautiful picture he envisioned, but now was not the time for painting such thoughts.

He led Blake's mother and daughter upstairs to the Med-Surg floor and found her room. She was wrapped in a white blanket, and IVs dripped down lines that flowed into her arm. Her eyes were closed and her hair billowed out around her head on the pillow. If it hadn't been for the monotonous beep of the machines hooked to her body, it would have looked as though she was just in a restful slumber.

"You okay, Meg?" he asked.

She nodded, but she was biting her lip and there was a slight sheen of tears at the corners of her eyes. He wished he could shelter her from seeing her mother like this, but there was nothing he could do. Todd had hurt so many people he loved.

Megan walked to the end of the bed. She reached out and touched her mother's toes, so softly that it looked as though she were reaching for a porcelain doll that at any moment could crack under the weight of her fingertips.

Blake opened her eyes and smiled. "You're here." She looked to Megan and then toward him. "I'm sorry."

Her words struck him. How, in a moment like this—where she could have lived or died—could she have anything to be sorry for?

"No, Blake," he started. "I should never have put you in danger. I—" *I love you.* He stopped before he finished his thought. She needed to focus on her family and not his feelings. "I'm glad you're awake."

Blake's smile disappeared, and she grimaced. Reaching up with her uninjured arm, she touched her side where they had removed the bullet.

All his daydreams and hopes slipped from him as he watched her writhe in pain. She was hurting because of his screwup. He should have taken the bullets. He should have made her stand back. He could have saved her from getting hurt—yet he had failed. He couldn't fail her again.

"If you need me, give me a call." He stepped toward the door.

He had to take himself out of the equation. The only way he could keep her safe was by distancing himself from her life.

Chapter Sixteen

All night the monitors at the nurse's station had beeped and rung, footsteps had echoed up and down the halls and occasionally there had been the sounds of crying from other patients' rooms. Blake had barely slept; the only reprieve came when the pain meds she'd been given forced her to succumb to a fitful slumber. As morning rose, and the sounds of the day filled the ward, she was already dressed and waiting to go, her arm immobilized in a sling.

The nurses had been kind as they wheeled her to the front entrance, where her mother and daughter waited. Her mother's old Cadillac sat low, its shocks worn out from years of driving up and down the hilly landscape of Butte.

"Mom!" Megan ran up to her and gave her a gentle hug.

She tried to keep her emotions in check as she looked up at her daughter's smiling face, the freckles that adorned her cheeks and the excitement in her eyes. In a second, she could have lost everything—her daughter, her family, her life.

And for what?

Todd O'Brien had nearly succeeded in taking his own life. He had failed, but it didn't make it fair or just. There was no justice. No rectifying the situation. One person had died and she nearly could have…and she still didn't understand exactly why.

Who, or what, was driving this madness?

Was it the mayor? Was it Todd? Or was it someone else, someone who loved to manipulate and pull the strings of those around them who were stupid enough to do their bidding?

Was it all some game driven by greed and land grubbing as she and Jeremy had assumed, or was it something more?

Her mother stood beside the car door as the nurses loaded her inside like she was an invalid. Her body would heal. It would be fine. Her soul was a different story. It suddenly felt like everything she did in her work was useless. She was just stomping out fires; she wasn't changing anything for the better. She wasn't making a difference like she had assumed she would when she had joined the force. She was just another cog in the wheel of an imperfect society.

For so long she'd been trying to fight the inequity she felt at being a woman in a male-dominated profession in small-town Butte. Looking back, she couldn't say that her fight had all been worth it. Everything felt so...asinine. All that really mattered was family and those that she loved.

Loved.

Her thoughts moved to Jeremy.

More than fulfilling her duties as a deputy, she was doing this for him. He needed his questions answered. She owed him the peace of mind that came with a murder solved.

If he cared so much, though, why wasn't he here?

"Where's Jeremy?" she asked her mother as they drove out of the parking lot and down the road that led to their house.

Her mother glanced over at her. There was a

look of trepidation on her face, as if she didn't want to tell her what she knew.

"What? Where is he?" Blake repeated.

"I don't know. He took this hard, you know," her mother said. "He was talking about going to Missoula, getting back to work."

"Why?"

Was he coming back? Had he given up on her? Why now, when she needed him the most, had he left her? Anger flooded her senses.

Her mother had said he'd taken the shooting hard, but if he could just leave her, that proved how little he cared.

She needed to solve this case so she never had to see his green eyes or his mischievous grin again. The doubts that she had been carrying with her about her ability to uncover the truth burned away.

The car pulled to a stop at a light. To her left

was a historic building she'd passed thousands of times. This time she stared at it. Its red bricks were starting to crumble at the corners, and the white paint that marked its entrance was bubbled and peeling with age. Most days she thought the building charming, a throwback to eras and worlds past…worlds built on the needs of society and people's unbreakable spirit. She thought of the person who'd built it. It must have been incredibly hard in those days. Butte had been nothing more than a rough-and-tumble mining town, yet the person behind the creation of the building had likely risked everything to see his dreams come true.

What had it once been? On the side of the building was a faded and weathered painting that read, "Sweet Candies." It shocked her. Someone had come to this town, where miners' lives were dominated by the dark, dirty world of inner earth, and he had decided what these men and their families needed more than anything was a brightly colored treat. It was beautiful in a poetic way.

No doubt the shop owner had likely faced adversity and ridicule for his dreams. Just like her. Yet he had found the strength to follow his dreams. Could she do the same?

The car lurched forward as the light changed. She had to get through this. She had to stop worrying about Jeremy and what others thought of her. She needed to focus on the investigation and nothing else; it was the only thing she could really control.

She thought back to Robert's house and the mine. Although she had spent hours in both places, she must have missed something. But what?

"Mom," she said, breaking the silence that

filled the car. "I need you to take me to the evidence unit."

"Blake," she said with an exacerbated sigh. "You can't go back to work. You just got out of the hospital. You need to go home, get some rest, and maybe you can come back in a few days."

The first forty-eight hours of an investigation were the most critical, and they had already passed that marker. If she didn't figure out everything she needed to know soon, it would become harder and harder to solve the crime.

"I need to find out who is behind all of this. It won't hurt me to look through paperwork, Mom."

"You already got Todd. What more do you need to do? You have your suspect."

Megan shifted in the backseat.

She couldn't stop now…not when she was so

close, not when she could find out—without a doubt—exactly what had led up to Robert's death and what role Todd had played.

"I'll only be a couple of hours. I'll call you to come get me when I'm done."

Her mother just looked at her.

"Hey, if nothing else, you'll know that I'm not going anywhere, right?" She tried to make light of the situation, but her mother didn't seem to appreciate the humor. It struck her how, even though she was a grown woman, her mother still wanted to protect her. Though they had their issues and disagreements, Gemma West truly loved her. That love was just like what Blake felt for her daughter—it was unwavering. "Everything will be fine, Mom. I promise."

A few minutes later, her mother parked in

front of the station. "I expect you to call me if you need anything."

Blake smiled. It was just like she was fifteen again and her mother was dropping her off at the school dance. But instead of resenting her as she had as a teenager, she loved her mother more for her concern. "I'll call you when I need you to pick me up."

She gave Megan a kiss on the forehead, and, as she leaned over, the stitches in her chest panged to life, reminding her of the damage her body had sustained. She pushed the pain away. "Be good. And take care of Grandma, okay?"

Megan nodded. When she looked up at Blake there was reservation in her eyes. She had seen that look before—when she had walked Megan into her first day of kindergarten, and when she had first left her baby to go back to work.

Her daughter didn't want her to go. That look broke her heart.

She stepped back toward the passenger's door, but her mother put her hand up, stopping her. "You go do your job," she said, looking back at Megan like she, too, had seen the look her daughter had given her. "I have Megan. We're going to have fun today. Aren't we, honey?"

"But, Grandma—" Megan started.

"Oh, come, now. I have an idea for a new quilt. Wouldn't you like to help me pick out some fabric?"

Megan's face took on that awkward look, the one that melded the excitement of youth with the reservations of a teenager.

"Thanks, Mom."

Gemma smiled, and in her eyes there was a shimmer of pride as if she knew exactly how much this case mattered to Blake.

Blake turned and made her way into the sheriff's department without looking back. Her mother was in control; she was the rock in their lives.

The mayor was walking away from her down the hall, and she hurried so he wouldn't see her. She wasn't sure she could face him right now. She rushed through the department and toward the evidence unit. She pressed the code into the keypad, and the door opened. She walked in—and found the unexpected. Sitting at the row of desks inside the area was Jeremy.

She stopped and stared at him, unsure of what to say.

He looked up, and his eyes widened with surprise. "What are you doing here? Why aren't you at the hospital?"

"They released me on good behavior," she said with a dry, cutting edge to her voice. "My mother told me you were going to Missoula. Why are you here? And how did you get in?"

There was a breath of warm air against the back of her neck. "I let him in," a man said.

She turned and standing there was Captain Prather.

"We needed someone to work on this case in your absence. Because of his experience as a detective and his gracious offer to act as a consultant, I brought him in. We need to solve this."

"You're absolutely right, sir." She turned around and moved toward the seat at the desk near Jeremy. "It's great that we have Todd O'Brien in custody."

"Blake," Captain Prather said, shaking his head, "before you sit down, we need to talk."

A cold chill tumbled down her spine. What was happening? Why was the captain looking at her with pity and disdain? Did it have something to do with the altercation with O'Brien? Sure, she had screwed up by getting in a shootout, but it was hardly her fault. She hadn't wanted things to end up that way.

She moved toward the captain. She glanced toward Jeremy, but he wouldn't meet her gaze. He knew something, something he couldn't tell her.

Was the ax about to fall?

"Sir…" she started, but she stopped herself. She couldn't bring herself to beg. She couldn't allow Jeremy to see her lose her cool.

Everything would be fine.

Captain Prather led her to his office and closed the door and the blinds. Whatever was about to happen was something he wanted no one else to know about.

He turned to her as he sat down in his chair. "Deputy West, take a seat."

She did as instructed. A cold sweat started to bead on her skin. He had used her formal title. This wasn't going to go well.

"I brought you in here today to talk about the altercation that occurred on Todd O'Brien's property last night."

That was no surprise.

"I'm highly disappointed in the events that transpired between you and Todd O'Brien."

"Captain, I—"

He shut her down with a raised finger. "I was depending on you to get a handle on this case. You knew what was at stake, yet you let it slip through your fingers—and, worse, you ended up getting hurt. This is going to come back on all of us, West."

"I know, sir, but we got Todd. We got our suspect."

"Your suspect? You think he was the one responsible for Robert Lawrence's murder? The murder that, according to you and the medical examiner, took place at approximately noon on Tuesday?"

She didn't like the way he spoke. Was she being set up to take a fall?

"Yes, sir." She looked down at her hands as she waited for his blow.

"If you would have checked into Todd O'Brien a little deeper, you would have realized that he was nowhere near Robert's claim on Tuesday morning. We have record of his credit card being used at the Missoula Costco at 11:15 a.m. and then the Cenex at 11:45."

"Sir, someone else could have used his credit

card." She was grasping at straws, and she knew it.

He nodded, but his body remained rigid, unwavering. "Jeremy's looking into the video footage from Costco to make sure that isn't the case. It is doubtful, however, that Todd is the person responsible for Robert's death."

The information came as a shock. What made it worse was the fact that Jeremy hadn't bothered to tell her.

"I...I did everything to the best of my abilities. Todd wasn't answering my questions. We were executing a search warrant. We would have found out the truth—"

"Mistakes in this game come at a high price, West."

"I know, sir. O'Brien made the choice to shoot. I just wanted to ask him some questions and search his property for evidence that linked him to the crime. I never wanted anyone to get hurt."

"I'm more than aware, from Jeremy Lawrence's testimony, that you may not be at fault for the events that occurred. That being said, however, there still must be a professional inquiry and investigation. Therefore, I must put you on paid administrative leave until things get figured out."

Her heart dropped. He was pulling her off the case.

She had lost what little reputation she had in the captain's eyes. She'd lost her chance to prove herself, and now it was likely she would lose her job. Everything she had fought so hard for… It was all gone.

Chapter Seventeen

Blake sat on the wooden bench outside the front of the station, waiting for her mother to come pick her up. She had been right. It was just like a high school dance—high hopes torn apart by the whips of reality that left her alone and once again calling her mother for help. This cycle was never going to end. No matter how badly she wanted to change.

Then again, maybe she was lucky to have a family like hers…a family that was always there. It may have been only her mother and her daughter, but they all had one another's backs. There was no question about loyalties or favorites. No turbulent marriage to worry about, like in Jeremy's family. Maybe that was why he couldn't trust, why he couldn't compromise. His family had to be the reason he was the way he was—for good and bad.

No matter how hard she tried to understand his actions, she couldn't come to terms with the fact that he had kept her in the dark. She had been in the hospital, but he could have come to see her and told her what he'd learned. It was her investigation. At least, it had been.

From the very beginning, he had strove to lead. The night in the mine, he had tried to tell her how to run the investigation. Was this just an extension of his need to control?

"That seat taken?" a man asked from behind her.

She turned to see Jeremy standing there. He

held his hands in front of him like a repentant child. If she hadn't been so angry, so hurt, he would have looked kind of cute the way his gaze fell to the ground and an apologetic smile lingered on his lips.

Lips she had kissed. Lips she had hoped to kiss again, but now she could barely look at.

She moved toward the middle of the small bench, taking both seats. It was juvenile, but she couldn't stand the thought of him being so close. She wasn't ready to have him near her, apologizing, trying to justify why he had done what he had done.

"Whatever you have to say, you can save it." She turned back and tried to focus on the torn blue awning that adorned the restaurant across the street.

He walked around and stood beside the

bench. "I know how this looks. But trust me—I didn't intend to get you in trouble."

"Then what exactly did you intend?"

She could smell the sandalwood and cloves of his cologne, but still she didn't look at him.

"I just wanted to dig up a little more information while I had the chance. I found something that I think will change everything."

"You mean the fact that Todd couldn't have been Robert's killer? Captain Prather already told me."

"I know, but I got something better."

Her head jerked up. "What?"

"I went back up to Todd's place after I knew you were okay. We found his tax records and a safe with land deeds. It looks like the guy at the bar was right. Todd was buying out the properties around him. He's the registered owner of almost all the land around the Foreman Mine.

Plus, I got the license plate of the car we saw under the tarp—the one you thought looked familiar. Turns out it's registered to Tiffany Lawrence."

"What? Why would Todd have Tiffany's car? Did you get a look inside?" she asked, moving over so he could sit down next to her.

He smiled as he took the spot next to her on the bench. "It looked pretty clean, but I had it towed to the evidence yard." He motioned toward the fenced compound that sat behind the sheriff's department.

"Did you have the techs go through it?"

"They're working on it now. You wanna—" He stopped and looked down at her sling, and his face tightened with concern. "You need to go home, West."

Her anger flared as he said her name like she

was just another deputy. "I don't need to do anything except finish my work on this case."

"I get it. You're trying to prove to the world that you can handle anything, but you don't have to be Superwoman, West."

"Stop calling me West like I'm some kind of stranger. We came this close," she said, pinching her fingers together, "to taking things too far. I've seen your skivvies."

He laughed, but the sound only made her more infuriated.

"What's so funny?"

"You said *skivvies*. Only my mother calls my underwear my skivvies."

"So now you're comparing me to your mother?" Her blood pressure rose. "I'm nothing like your mother. No matter how badly you want to live out some Freudian thing."

He stopped smiling. "That's not what I meant.

I didn't mean to make you mad. I just thought it was cute, that's all."

Leave it to a man to find her anger attractive, provocative even.

"If you think I'm so cute, why do you keep screwing with me? First, you want to run everything, and now you get me put on administrative leave and make me look like an idiot in front of my captain."

"It's no secret that I care about you, Blake." He said her name carefully.

"If you care about me, you have one screwed-up way of showing it." She gripped the cast-iron armrest of the antique-style bench.

"I'm trying to protect you."

She balked. "What? How are you protecting me by letting me get taken away from the job I love?"

"Do you really love your job?"

How dare he ask her a question like that? She loved her job. She went to it nearly every day and helped save the innocent. It wasn't the glorious, romantic job the television shows made it out to be, but it kept her and her family fed.

"Do you love *your* job?" She turned the question on him. "You say you're trying to help your family, but what is the truth, Jeremy? I heard about the case with the battalion chief. Was it weighing on your conscience? Was it why you needed to gain control of this investigation? Why you were happy to see me put on administrative leave?"

"I had nothing to do with your administrative leave. You know that. It's just your department's policy. I didn't write it. I don't enforce it. If I wanted to take over this case, then why in the hell would I be telling you about Tiffany's car?"

He made a point, but she wasn't mollified. "Why didn't you tell me about Robert's credit card statements and how they cleared him?"

"I didn't tell you because I only just found out. I haven't even had time to look into the video surveillance yet. Just because someone used his credit card doesn't mean that he was the one doing it."

"The captain seemed to think it was him."

"Your captain doesn't work the beat. I think it's just one hell of a convenient alibi that this guy who, according to his bank records, only shops at three places—the closest little family-run grocery store, the hardware store and the gun shop—all of a sudden branches out and goes to Costco in another town on the day of the murder. It's out of character for the guy."

"Do you think he went there just so he could be on tape?"

"It's one hell of a solid alibi if it works out

that way." Jeremy nodded. "But that's not why I think he did it. I think he believes your department is lazy and stupid."

She gave a light snort. It was like Todd to think he was smarter than her and the rest of the sheriff's department. He'd never tried to hide his disdain for law enforcement. And with that level of egocentric behavior came the belief that he could get away with anything.

"I bet he thought we'd never look into the video surveillance. That we'd just take the statements at face value and go no deeper," Jeremy said. "Maybe that's why he was so jumpy when we executed the warrant. Maybe he thought he'd been caught."

She sat there in silence digesting everything that Jeremy was saying. Was he right? Was that the reason that Todd had pulled the gun? That he had been desperate enough to try to take his own life? For the first time, it started to make sense.

"If he wasn't the one to go to Costco, then who do you think it was?"

Jeremy glanced over toward the evidence lot. "I don't know for sure, but I think we need to start looking for Tiffany."

The door opened behind them, and the desk sergeant came rushing out. "West?" He hurried toward her.

"What is it?" she asked, jumping to her feet.

"There's been a report." He looked nervous, wringing his hands, and there was a line of sweat in the furrow on his brow.

"About?" she pressed, trying to help the struggling man find his words.

"There's been a fire…a fire at your house."

JEREMY'S TIRES SQUEALED as Blake took the corner entirely too fast. Safety and speed limits were for people whose families weren't in danger. She screeched to a stop behind the fire trucks that blocked the road. She slammed the door as she got out and started sprinting up the hill to her house.

"Blake, wait!" Jeremy called as he got out after her.

From the moment the desk sergeant had told her about the fire, she'd seemed to completely forget he was with her. She'd grabbed his car keys off the bench, gotten behind the wheel and screeched out, giving him no choice but to scoot into the passenger's seat or be left behind. Nothing else had mattered. Nothing but Megan and her mother. They needed her.

Jeremy ran, catching up to her. "You can't just charge in there. There will need to be an investigation."

"I don't care about any investigation. I need

to know Megan's okay," she said between breaths as she ran.

As Blake crested the hill, she saw her. Megan's blond hair, her cheeks covered in a light smattering of ash and her eyes red from tears. Gemma was beside her, holding her, but she let go as Blake approached.

"It's okay. Everything's okay," her mother said, as if she could see the terror that Blake was feeling.

Blake threw her arms around Megan and, pushing back her hair, inspected her face. There was no burns, no marks other than the smudges of ash. "Are you okay?"

"I'm fine, Mom," Megan said, wiping a tear from her cheek.

"What happened?" Jeremy asked. "Are you okay, Mrs. W?"

The older woman nodded. "Oh, it wasn't

anything serious. Just a little fire in the yard. Everything's fine." She motioned toward the front yard where the fire crews were dousing the stunted pine with water. The pitch-filled, stubborn tree was still smoldering, spitting and hissing as they tried to force it into submission.

Blake laughed, the sound high, maniacal. The movement made her side hurt and the stitches burn in her flesh, but the pain did nothing to subdue her hysteria.

"What's so funny?" her mother asked, sounding confused.

She tried to stop laughing so she could answer her, but fate's cruel joke was more than she could bear.

Jeremy moved closer to her, took her in his arms and, careful of her wound, hugged her. His kindness made tears well in her eyes. She tried to blink them away. It was just stress that was making her lose it like this. Just stress. She needed to pull herself together, to be strong for Megan.

She stopped laughing, swallowing the sound like it was a bitter pill. She moved to step out of Jeremy's arms, to show the world that she could keep her emotions in check, but she stopped. His warmth felt so good. His scent had changed slightly and now carried a rich scent of fear and panic. He must have felt as she did. Yet here he was, the person trying to hold her together. Why did he have to be so strong all the time?

She wanted to resent him for his strength, to hate him for the confusing mess of emotions that he made her feel, but she couldn't…not now, not when it felt so right to be in his arms. He may not love her, but he cared for her. It was foreign, to be really cared for by a man. Not even her own father had really loved her, or at least it hadn't seemed that way when he'd run away from their family when she was young.

Jeremy looked at her. Their eyes met. There was a light in his that she had seen once before—the night in Robert's cabin. She had to be wrong. He didn't want to be with her. He was only a friend—a friend she was giving entirely too much of her heart to.

She stepped out of his arms and readjusted her sling more out of nervousness than need.

"Ma'am?" one of the firefighters asked as he came up to her. "Are you the home owner?"

She looked to her mother. "We are."

He nodded. "We think we have the fire under control. However, we located a couple of things that we think you should take a look at."

"Will you guys be okay here?" she asked her mother and Megan. Her mother drew Megan back into her arms, the girl coming up almost to her shoulders.

It was shocking to see how much older her daughter seemed than only just a few days ago. It was like she had gone through a transformation in front of Blake's eyes. Or perhaps, it wasn't her daughter who had transformed but rather Blake herself. Maybe for the first time she was really seeing the world around her for the way that it was—ever changing and evolving.

She stepped over to her daughter and kissed her forehead.

"Mom, are you okay?" Megan asked, looking up at her.

"I'm fine. I'm sorry for laughing."

"Why *were* you laughing?" her mother asked. "Stress?"

"Yes, but it…" She looked to Jeremy. "I always thought that tree was just like me."

Her mother frowned with confusion as she glanced over in the direction of the tree. "I don't get it."

Blake smiled as she patted her mother's shoulder. "It's okay. Just know that I love you, Mom."

She turned and walked away, Jeremy following behind.

Her feet sloshed in the wet grass and mud of the front yard. The fire had moved down the tree and set the grass at its base ablaze, but the crew had done a good job in controlling its progression. The tree was blackened, but its bark was still twisting with serpentine orange embers that slithered into the light and then disappeared.

"What did you mean about the tree?" Jeremy asked as they stopped in front of it.

"For years, this damn thing has been struggling to survive here in this poisoned city. It tried to grow but was always held back by the chemicals that had leeched into its roots. See the way it twists there?" she asked, pointing toward a burl in the trunk. "When my father left, he was so drunk he backed the car into it. My mother wanted to cut it down, but I wouldn't let her. I loved and hated that tree, but I wanted it to survive."

Jeremy took her hand in his. "You were wrong about the tree being just like you."

She looked to him, confused.

The fireman motioned to them to follow him behind the tree. "We found this," he said, pointing at the ground.

In the unburned grass was a blackened plastic

doll. Its face had melted, but the arms and legs were still discernible. A little tuft of charred red hair stuck out from the back of the doll's head. Even disfigured, Blake recognized it as one of Megan's favorite old dolls—the one from the bookshelf in her room.

Someone had been in their house long enough to find something personal and use it against them. That someone had meant to instill fear. And it worked. But more than fear rose within Blake. In addition, there was an onslaught of rage at the thought that someone had had the gall to violate their home. Not just their home, but specifically her innocent daughter's bedroom.

Who would have done such a thing? And why?

"There's something else, as well," the fireman said as he started walking toward the side of the house.

Sprayed on the siding in orange paint was a message.

DEATH AWAITS YOU

The hair on her arms rose.

"There was also a note," he said, pointing toward a white sheet of paper that was pinned to the wall.

She moved close so that she could read the words.

If you don't leave Butte, I will kill you and your family. Run, if you know what is good for you.

She slipped her hand from Jeremy's as she moved to tear down the letter, but she stopped herself. This was evidence. Evidence they could use.

"We're in luck," Jeremy said.

"How is getting a death threat lucky?" she asked, tilting her head toward the hateful note.

"Whoever wrote this doesn't know me."

"How's that?" she asked.

"You know Casper?" Jeremy smiled.

She was totally lost. "What about your brother?"

"Before he went to work for the US Border Patrol, he used to work for the FBI…as a hand-writing analyst. If I call him, I bet he can have his findings back to us within a few hours. He can help us bring down this sucker. And when I get my hands on them, they'll wish they never lived."

Chapter Eighteen

Jeremy tapped his pencil on the kitchen table. He hated waiting. He hated being forced into inaction. But right now he was waiting for a lead. A lead only his brother Casper could give them, once his handwriting analysis was completed.

In the meantime, his mother kept coming in and out of the kitchen; by now she must have been on her eighth cup of tea.

"Is there anything I can help you guys with?" she asked.

Blake looked up and Jeremy saw the dark circles that had started to form under her eyes as the night descended on them. She wiggled in the wooden chair as if her injuries were bothersome.

"You need something, Blake?" he asked. "Ibuprofen or something? You look like you're getting sore."

Blake shook her head. "I'm fine—they're nothing more than flesh wounds," she said, trying to make it sound like a joke, but from the slow edge to her speech he could tell she was hurting.

"Where're her painkillers, Mom?" he asked, standing up.

She went to the cupboard next to the sink and retrieved the bottle.

"Thanks." He took out a couple of pills, then filled up a glass of water and handed them to Blake. "Take these."

"I told you…it's nothing," she argued.

"You don't have to be tough in front of me. I know how bad you have to be hurting right now." As he said it, he suddenly realized that it was likely her body wasn't hurting half as badly as her spirit was.

There was little worse than having one's home violated. Thankfully, she and her family had agreed to take his and his brother's old bedrooms. It was the least he could do to make sure that they stayed safe.

"Is Megan asleep?" he asked.

His mother nodded. "Yeah, she passed right out."

Blake looked at him. "Thanks again for letting us crash here. I'm sure we would have been fine at our place, but it's nice having—" She stopped before finishing her sentence.

Was she going to say that it was nice having him around? Or had she meant something else?

They had their ups and downs, but he couldn't help the way he felt about her. They were more than friends but less than lovers. Yet the more time they spent together, the more he was willing to give up a few things in his life. Maybe. He could never leave Missoula. He loved his job. He doubted that she would be willing to leave Butte. Her family had been born and raised here; her past was here.

His thoughts moved to the night her father had stormed out of her house. He'd been drunk and slammed his car into the tree. After that night, he'd never seen the man again…and from what he'd heard from his mother, neither had Blake.

Maybe the past could be a reason she would want to leave.

He hated to get his hopes up that she would be willing to change her life for him. The only thing she had been willing to give him lately was a piece of her mind. Not that he blamed her.

If she wanted this like he did, there would have to be compromises on both sides. And compromising had never been one of his strong suits.

He looked toward his mother. "What about Mrs. W?"

"She's watching a little television. I'll go keep her and your father company," she answered, swirling the tea bag around in her cup.

As the door to the kitchen swung shut, his phone rang. It was Casper.

"What did you find?" Jeremy asked, trying to keep his nervous excitement in check.

"It's nice to talk to you, too, snotface," his brother chided.

"Yeah, yeah. If I wanted an etiquette lesson I would ask for help from Dear Abby."

His brother laughed, reminding Jeremy just how much he missed him…and, regardless of the animosity they had held for each other, how much he would miss Robert now that he was gone.

"So you're taking on Robert's case?" Casper asked, almost as if he could tell by the silence what Jeremy was thinking about.

"Yeah. Helping out our former neighbor, Blake West."

"I remember Blake," Casper said, his voice filled with the excitement that came with reminiscing. "She still hot?"

"Uh…" Jeremy looked over at Blake. His cheeks warmed, and he tried to staunch his blushing. For the first time that evening, she smiled. "She's as beautiful as ever."

She looked away as her features seemed to take on a reddish hue of their own.

"I'll have to check her out when I come down for Robert's services. You know when they are going to release the body?"

"Probably not until we get a handle on the murder. Speaking of...did you find anything in the handwriting analysis?" He set the phone down and put it on speaker.

"I don't know what you were expecting, but I did find some interesting things in the note." Casper paused, and there was the sound of rustling papers on the other end of the line. "If you take a look at the physical characteristics and the pattern in the note, the letters are almost at a forty-five-degree angle, and they're jagged, rushed. Whoever did this was in a hurry, but they were likely driven by passion or anger."

If they were in a hurry, they had likely written

it on-scene. Which meant they knew there was a chance of being seen. Yet they had thought that their mission was worth the danger.

"Looking closer, whoever wrote it was a woman."

"A woman?" he repeated, shocked by his brother's claim. "How do you know that?"

"If you look at the loops and swirls in the handwriting, it's distinctly feminine. And, based on the angle of her letters, she's left-handed."

"Left-handed, huh?" His thoughts moved to the fingerprint the tech had found on the gun.

"Did you find out anything about Tiffany yet?" Casper asked, his voice full of suspicion.

"No, but we're going to use all available resources until we do. Dead or alive, we need to know if she's involved in this."

Jeremy looked to Blake, his eyes conveying

his conviction. He couldn't help noticing her eyeliner was smudged and bits of mascara had flaked onto her cheeks. Even slightly disheveled, she was still the most beautiful woman he'd ever seen.

"Thanks, Casper."

"No problem. And hey," Casper added, "if you need me, I can be there within a few hours."

"No worries. Blake and I can handle this," he said, never breaking eye contact with her. "We can handle anything."

BLAKE TWITCHED AS the brothers spoke of time, the measurement of everything in her world. Yet now the only time that really mattered was the mounting hours that had slipped by since Robert's murder. With every passing second, the chances of their solving this case were going up in smoke.

She stood up and grabbed the uniform jacket she'd hung on the coatrack by the door. "Ready?"

Jeremy looked up at her. "For what?"

"We need to get out there. Get a line on Tiffany."

He glanced at his watch. "It's almost eleven o'clock at night. Where do you think we can go that we're going to find her at this hour? First, we don't know if she's even the woman behind the fire. There's no direct evidence of her being involved. Second, we haven't heard anything about her whereabouts since the start of this investigation."

"What other woman, besides Tiffany, would care if we're investigating your brother's murder?"

"Blake, the note never mentioned the investigation. It was a death threat, nothing more. For all we know, it was just some whack-job who's been reading the paper and got it in her head that you're the devil. Who knows?"

Blake gripped her jacket so hard that her fingers on her good hand throbbed. "You wouldn't feel the same way if it was you or your family being threatened. You're minimizing this."

"I can assure you I'm not. I'm just as upset about what happened as you are, but you need to rest. When the sun comes up, you and I can go full-on guns blazing, but tonight you should take a break and let your body heal. You're no good to anyone if you end up back in the hospital because you've refused to take care of yourself."

He was right, but it didn't lessen the urgency she felt. Whoever thought they could come into her house and threaten her family needed to pay.

Jeremy stood up slipped her coat over her

shoulders. "Why don't we go for a walk and get some air?"

She nodded, glad that he hadn't attempted to calm her by requesting she stay put. This was one of those times when the only thing that was going to make her better was the feel of pavement under her feet.

He opened the door and followed her outside. The night air was brisk and had started to take on the smell of fading leaves and the last blooms of the season.

They made their way down the sidewalk and started down the hill. The full moon lit their way, and far off in the distance atop a mountain was a white sculpture called *Our Lady of the Rockies*.

"Did you know that she is dedicated to mothers everywhere?" Blake asked, pointing up at the woman atop the mountain.

"You ever been up there?"

She shook her head. There were hiking tours and helicopter rides that went up to the ninety-foot statue, but she'd never been.

"You can see the Berkeley Pit and the entire city. It's hard not to think about all the people who gave their lives for this corrupt place."

"Who owns the mines around the pit?" Jeremy asked.

"The one and only Tartarus Environmental Investments—headed by our glorious mayor. They shut down the mines in the 1990s. I think they weren't making enough money per yard to keep the large-scale mines running. Ever since then they've been hurting for money."

They had cleared the mayor as a suspect, but she couldn't help the nagging feeling that he was still somehow connected.

They walked in silence, their footfalls and

the occasional passing car the only sounds. Jeremy reached over and took Blake's hand, and his heat soaked into her cold fingers. It was wonderful to have a man want to touch her, to reach out and take her hand not with ownership but rather something deeper, more visceral… more caring.

She glanced down at their entwined fingers. For a moment she couldn't tell where he stopped and she began. Noticing her attention, he ran his thumb over the back of her hand, stoking her desire.

"Do you think Mayor Engelman is involved in all this?" she asked him.

He nodded. "There's something so wrong about him. It has to be more than circumstantial that all of a sudden Robert gets a tax lien. Then he ends up dead…and the mayor's company is there to scoop up the claim. I just wish we could find concrete evidence to tie him to this thing. Something he can't deny."

They walked slowly up the hill that led to Montana Tech's School of Mines and Engineering. The brick buildings in front of them acted as sentinels as they approached. On the side of one was a picture of a man wearing a hard hat and holding a pickax, and above him read Go Orediggers.

The small college campus was eerily quiet. There were a few cars parked in the lots, but there wasn't a single student hurrying across the grass or making his or her way back to the dorms. As silent and desolate as the campus seemed, it was a comfort. The last thing she wanted right now was to share the silence with anyone other than Jeremy.

There were a few lights on in the buildings, but most were black and closed down for the night. Near the edge of the campus was a gazebo nestled in bushes and covered in yellow roses. Jeremy let go of Blake's hand and made his way over to them, breaking one off. He came back to her and handed her the flower. Its heady fragrance filled her senses.

"That's sweet, thanks," she said, twirling the open bud in her fingers.

"I hope you know how bad I feel…about everything."

"The fire wasn't your fault," she said, taking another sniff of the flower.

"That's not what I mean. I mean I'm sorry for *everything*," he said, looking into her eyes. In the moonlight, his eyes appeared as if they were full of stars. He took the rose from her and slipped it behind her ear.

She could hold a grudge, but after everything that had happened over the past few days she didn't have the energy to deny her true feelings. He was nice to have around, and it was nice to have someone who wanted to help her, someone she could trust.

He stepped up into the gazebo and disappeared behind the roses. She followed him up the steps and sat down on the bench at the center. He walked over to her and gently put his hands on her shoulders. She reached up with her good hand and placed it on his. The concrete had started to cool in the night air. A chill moved through her, but she wasn't sure if it was the cold or Jeremy's nearness.

"I never wanted you to get hurt," he said, running his finger over the strap of her sling. "I never wanted you to feel threatened."

She looked up at him, and her lips brushed against his arm. She paused and let the sensation of his soft hairs against her skin sink into her. Ever so gently, she leaned her face against his arm and let herself just feel his touch.

"I made my choices, Jeremy. I've known ever since I chose this path that it was possible I could get hurt. What happened at Todd's wasn't your fault. I froze."

"You shouldn't have been taking point."

She didn't want to argue with him, not when he was looking at her like he was searching for forgiveness and maybe something more. He touched her face, soft at first, unsure. Taking his hands in hers, she kissed his palm. She stood up as she ran her lips down the length of his finger and took the tip of it into her mouth and sucked. His breath hitched, and his body tensed with anticipation.

Moving into him, she pressed against his body and traced his wet finger across the curve of her lip, over her chin and down her neck.

"I'm not the kind of woman who is going to stand back and let others get what I want."

He looked at her as he played with one of her loose hairs, wrapping it around his finger and unwrapping it as if he was in a daze.

"What is it that you want?"

"Right now?" she asked, her breath catching in her throat as she admitted what she had repressed for so long. "Right now, I want you."

He took her lips. His kiss was hard and hungry. He tasted of salt and the sweetness of desire. Jeremy wanted this. He wanted this as badly as she did.

Wrapping his arms around her, he led her to the concrete column behind them, pressing her body against the cold stone. It made the heat of his kiss more intense, and her body throbbed with lust.

He stopped and looked down at her sling. "Are you sure you are okay? You can do this?"

She answered with a seductive smile. There was no possible way she was going to pass up on her chance to be with Jeremy. This may be the last time they could be together. He would go back to Missoula as soon as their investigation was over, and once again she would be alone. At least this way she could be left with the memory of their time together.

One by one she undid his buttons, making her way down his shirt and exposing his chest. She felt his muscles tighten as she moved lower and ran her fingers over the ridges of his perfect body.

"I only need one good hand," she said, slipping her hand in the waistband of his pants until she found her target.

She took control of him and stroked his

length. He threw his head back and pulled in a ragged breath as she moved.

After a moment, his hard, hot hand stilled hers and he withdrew it. Giving as he got, he reached down and unfastened her pants. Sliding the fabric down her thighs, he let them fall to the stone. He took off his shirt and laid it on the ground. The muscles of his chest were highlighted by the moon, making him seem mystical, like a Greek god who had come to her in the night.

Ever so gingerly, he laid her on his shirt and pulled her panties down her legs, kissing her skin as they inched lower.

She relished the feel of his moist breath and the tender movement of his kiss, but as she looked around she suddenly remembered where they were.

"Don't you think we should hurry? What if

someone sees us?" she said, her voice breath-less and drunken with want.

He looked up at her from between her thighs. "I've wanted this…and you…for too long to want to rush."

Reaching up, he pulled the rose from behind her ear. Ever so slowly, he traced the velvet pet-als over her legs, kissing each place the flower brushed. He ran the petals toward the heat at her center. As his lips moved up her thigh, she forgot her apprehension.

His tongue fluttered against her, light at first but stroke by stroke his mouth drove harder against her, making her body feel as though she would fall to pieces under the pleasure of his touch.

"No," she whispered, though her body begged her to say only yes. She ran her fingers through his hair as he looked up from between her thighs. "I want to feel you… All of you."

He leaned down and kissed her, making her tremble with lust.

"Please," she begged.

He smiled as he looked at her, his eyes mirroring her want and he moved up between her thighs.

"I'm yours… I've wanted you… This… Always." He drove himself inside of her with just the right mix of gentleness and force.

He moved inside of her, her body rising to his. She shifted her hips, pulling him deeper. Their bodies moved together until she wasn't sure exactly who was who. The world disappeared as he laced his fingers through her hair and took her lips.

Her body parted for him, taking all of him,

wanting all of him…needing everything he could give.

She wanted this moment to last. Yet her breath caught in her throat as her body disobeyed her mind.

"Jeremy…" she whispered, her voice urgent and telling of what her body promised.

"Yes," he said, his mouth caressing her earlobe. "Yes, be mine."

She let herself go as he drove hard and fast inside of her.

Stars flecked her vision and, as Jeremy's body mimicked hers, for a moment she wasn't sure if something that felt so glorious and right could be real.

Jeremy lowered his body, letting his head fall to her chest as if he wanted to listen to the sounds of her heart. She held him, running her fingers dazedly over the muscles of his shoulders and through his hair.

She had waited for so long for this moment, if only it could last forever.

Chapter Nineteen

Jeremy wasn't the type to smile like an idiot, but he couldn't help the contented grin that had taken over his face and made his cheeks grow sore. He couldn't believe how lucky he was, at least for one night.

He held Blake's hand as they crested the hill that led back to his parents' place. As they approached, the front porch light was on, but inside the house was dark. He was a bit relieved. There was no way he could have hidden what had happened and the giddiness he felt.

Making love with Blake was everything he'd

hoped it would be. And he never wanted it to end. But he knew it must. She needed to rest, and they had a case they needed to get back to in the morning. A case riddled with questions.

As if she read his mind, she asked him one. "When you guys went back to Todd's place, did you find any evidence of a woman living at his property?"

"Why?"

"What if Tiffany had been living with Todd? Maybe she had been there, hiding out. Maybe that was what Todd was hiding."

It made sense. If Blake was right, it was no wonder that Todd wanted nothing to do with them or their investigation.

"Was Todd's truck still there?"

He frowned. "I don't think so."

"Then I think we need to put an APB out on his truck. If we find it, we may find Tiffany."

OVERNIGHT A LATE-SUMMER storm had rolled in. The gray, ominous clouds that had dampened the earth still loomed overhead, threatening more rain. They had been making phone calls all day, tracking down Tiffany's friends, and they had gotten their first solid lead when they had called a woman named Judith. She had sounded concerned about her friend's disappearance, but there had also been an edge of panic in her voice that made Blake want to reach out and talk in person with the woman.

The truck sloshed through the mud puddles, kicking up fat droplets of muck onto the windshield as Jeremy bumped down the road that led to Tiffany's best friend's house.

Despite her administrative leave, Blake had refused to be left out of this investigation. It felt strange to not have her badge on her chest. Yet with or without her badge, she had to protect her family, and the only way she knew how was by stopping whomever had threatened them. It had been painful to watch as Megan had spent the morning cautiously lurching around the house, looking out the windows toward their home and talking about the threat. Megan had wanted to go home, but the idea hadn't been discussed. They needed the relative safety of Jeremy's parents' place.

Jeremy's mother had seemed almost excited at the prospect of others helping to keep her from her routine with her husband, though she still gave the man the side-eye every time they were in the same room together.

As long as she could remember, the Lawrences had always had a turbulent relationship, but with Robert's death it was doubtful that their marriage would survive. The resentment that surfaced after a child died, even an adult child, rarely brought a couple together. In all honesty, it was a wonder they were still married, but it made sense as to why Jeremy seemed to steer away from anything approaching a relationship—with the exception of last night.

She licked her lips. She could almost still taste his kiss.

Looking over at him as he talked on the phone, she watched as his mouth moved. The simple action made her warm with lust as she thought of all the places his lips had traveled in the moonlight.

Jeremy hung up and turned his attention back to the road. "I told Judith we'd be there in less than five minutes. You get an update on the APB on Todd's truck?"

She shook her head. No one had seen the truck or the woman they were looking for. It was like they were chasing a phantom—and maybe they were. If Tiffany Lawrence was dead, their investigation was, as well. Even though they could prove Todd was land grubbing, there was no proof that he had killed Robert. They had only a few leads, and even fewer people who seemed to have any usable information.

This was her last hope to save her career. If they didn't solve this case, she had no doubt that not only would she be fired from the department; it was unlikely that she would ever be hired in law enforcement again. She would end up right where she had started, a single mother without a dependable income, left to find a path in life that would keep her and her family above water.

"You okay?" Jeremy reached over and touched

her neck, gently stroking his strong, callused thumb over her skin.

She melted at his touch. "Absolutely."

Her mother would have called out her lie in an instant, but Jeremy just looked at her. Perhaps he didn't know she was lying, or else he had decided to delve no further. Either way he remained silent as they slogged down the road.

They pulled to a stop in front of a big, beautiful log cabin and walked up the slate path. The impressive structure had a green metal roof and a hand-carved alder front door complete with a horse's head door knocker. The place oozed wealth.

She pressed the doorbell, and chimes sounded. A woman in a black maid's uniform answered the door. In all of her life, this was the last kind of place she would have expected to find a friend of Tiffany's. The last time Blake had seen Tiffany, she had been strung out on liquor and taking wide, drunken swings at her husband. To say she was an alcoholic was an understatement. But was it possible that Blake had gotten her all wrong? Had she just seen the woman at her low point, the recipient of a ticket for disturbing the peace?

"May I help you?" the maid asked, looking them up and down.

"We're here to ask the lady of the house a few questions about Tiffany Lawrence. Is she around?" Jeremy asked. He looked as taken aback as she was at the juxtaposition between Tiffany's lifestyle and her best friend's, but he kept quiet.

The maid looked back over her shoulder. "I can see if she's available, sir." The door clicked shut behind her as she left them standing there to wait.

"Are you sure we have the right place?" Blake asked.

Jeremy shrugged. "I got this woman's name from my mother. She said she had seen Tiffany and this Judith woman running around as thick as thieves."

"But your mother didn't tell you she was loaded?"

He shook his head as the front door opened and a slim blonde stood before them. Her perfectly coifed hair reminded Blake of one of the cover models that adorned *Vogue*.

"How do you do, ma'am," Jeremy said, acting the gentleman. "Do you mind if we come in?"

The woman nodded and motioned for them to follow her inside. Her stilettos tapped on the marble floors, echoing in the cavernous entrance. "I'm so glad you called. I've been so worried about Tiffany," she said, her voice carrying the lilt of the well educated. "Is it true that she may have been murdered?" She stopped walking as they entered the living room and turned to face them.

"We aren't at liberty to discuss that, ma'am," Jeremy answered.

For some reason, Blake couldn't help the feeling of jealousy that crept through her. Just because the woman was well kept, skinny and beautiful didn't mean that Jeremy wanted her. Though, admittedly, he was being more formal than she had ever seen him. Her jealousy grew, making an angry knot form in her stomach.

"Are you friends with Mrs. Lawrence, Mrs...." Blake waited for a moment as the woman looked her over.

"It's Ms. Judith Davy," the woman said, thumbing the heavy-looking diamond and matching wedding band on her left hand.

Of course she was a Davy. Marcus Davy had been one of the founders of the mines in their city. It made perfect sense that the woman before them would be related.

She glanced over at Jeremy, but he seemed focused on the massive river rock fireplace that ran from the ceiling to the floor of the living room.

"Nice painting," he said, motioning above the mantel at an oil painting of an elk bugling as it stood in a running brook. Snowy mountain peaks dotted the background.

"Thanks, it's my husband's. He's more of an outdoorsman than I am. Tiffany and I bonded over that," she said, perching on the edge of the leather sofa. She motioned for them to take a seat across from her.

"What do you mean you bonded over that?" Blake sat down. The pedestal of the coffee table between them was a bronze statue that looked like fish swimming through a stream.

Ms. Davy adjusted the cuffs of her sweater. "Well, Miss—"

"It's Deputy West," Blake said, once again wishing she was wearing her uniform.

"Excuse me, *Deputy* West," Judith said with the raise of an eyebrow as she looked at Blake's department-store button-down white blouse.

Jeremy looked over at her and frowned. "Anyway," he said, turning back to Ms. Davy, "how would you classify your friendship with Tiffany?"

The woman relaxed a bit, easing back into the safety of her sofa. "Tiffany and I have been friends for a long time now. She loves to come over. We often shop for antiques together."

The tale screamed foul. Tiffany had always seemed more likely to take methamphetamines than to spend a day shopping, but Blake remained quiet. Maybe Tiffany had been a social chimera—able to spend the days in the mine alongside her husband, and in her off time climb the ladder of high society.

"Have you been in contact with Tiffany lately?" Jeremy asked.

"I heard about what happened to her husband. I tried to call her the other day, after I heard, but she didn't answer." The woman's face contorted as if she was angry with herself for talking to them.

Everything about this place and this woman felt wrong.

"Had you talked to her in the days before you heard about Robert's death?" Blake pressed.

The woman glanced to her left. "Absolutely not."

The woman was lying. Blake could hear it in

her inflection. It was the same sound she had made when she had lied to Jeremy. The sound was too high, the air too flippant. She was certain Ms. Davy was a fraud.

"When was the last time you talked to her?" Jeremy continued.

Blake moved toward him and was going to signal him that it was time to go, but she held back.

"I talked to Tiffany about a week ago. My husband and I had invited her and Robert over for supper. Unfortunately, at the last minute, Todd couldn't make it."

"Who did you say your husband was, Ms. Davy?" Blake asked.

The woman looked over at her and smiled. Her teeth were long and sharp, and she reminded Blake of a tiger. "My husband? Oh, his name's John."

"John Davy? Like the golfer?" Blake asked.

The woman laughed, the high sound stinging her ears. "Close, that's John Daly. No, I didn't take my husband's name when we got married. My husband is the mayor…Mayor John Engelman."

"He's your *husband*?" Blake tried to sound assertive, but her voice came out as a breathless squeak.

Judith smiled, her tigerlike fangs reappearing. "Are you friends of his?"

Blake bit her tongue so hard she could taste the iron-rich flavor of blood.

"We're acquainted. He was at the shooting competition the other day—is that correct?" Jeremy asked.

The woman gave a shrill laugh. "Oh, yes. We hired him to make a speech at the finals."

"*You* hired him?"

"Not me, but I'm on the board for the Montana Handgun Association."

"You're a sharpshooter?" Jeremy leaned forward, tenting his fingers in front of him like he was calling forth the beast.

She laughed. "I'm decent with a gun, but it's just a hobby—you know, something to give me a break from work."

"What kind of work is it that you do, Ms. Davy?"

"I'm the CFO for my husband's company, Tartarus Environmental Investments." Her phone rang and she hurried across the room to pick it up. She answered it, saying something in what Blake assumed was Japanese.

She must have asked the caller to hold, because she lowered the phone and turned to them. "Detective, Deputy, I'm afraid I can't be any more help in your attempt to find Tiffany. I need to get back to my work. I'm sure you know how it is." She forced a smile as she lifted her phone like it was evidence of her business, but there was a new strain in the way she moved, as if it was crucial they leave.

"We understand," Jeremy said, holding out his hand to help Blake stand. He gave it a light squeeze, reassuring her that she wasn't alone in her suspicion.

Every cell in her body screamed for her to slap her cuffs on the woman and take her straight to jail, but there wasn't room for any more mistakes. Judith was a powerful and dangerous woman.

Chapter Twenty

Blake reached over and turned on the heat in the truck, but no amount of warmth would dispel Jeremy's numbness. How could they have missed this earlier? There had been so many lines running to the mayor, so many motivations to get Robert's land and mineral rights. Yet they had written him off. They'd never thought to check out his wife. Was she the killer they had been looking for all along?

Judith hardly seemed like the type who could walk up to his brother and put a round in his head, but if he'd learned one thing in his years as a detective, it was that killers looked like everyone else. If anything, a killer was more likely to be the innocent-looking neighbor rather than the schizophrenic transient. It was always the ones that people didn't see coming that ended up being the most dangerous—and the hardest to pin down.

Blake looked over at him and shook her head. "What are we going to do?"

He swallowed back the lump in his throat. "It's more important than ever that we find Tiffany. We need someone…anyone…who can help us figure out what in the hell is going on."

Blake nodded, but her lips were pursed like she knew exactly how unlikely it was that Tiffany would hold the answers they needed. "Ms. Davy was definitely in a rush to get us out of her house. Who do you think she was talking to?"

"No idea, but something was up."

His phone rang, the sound making him jump. "This is Lawrence," he answered.

"This is Sergeant McDonald with the Montana Highway Patrol. I'm just outside of Butte and I believe I have a truck pulled over that matches your description. I have taken the driver into custody. How would you like me to proceed?"

He pulled over, the truck's tires sliding in the muddy grit on the side of the road.

"Do you have an ID on the driver?"

"The woman doesn't have any form of identification, but she says her name is Sophia Lawrence."

Lawrence? It had to be Tiffany. "What does the woman look like?"

"Dark hair, about one hundred sixty-five pounds, and a tattoo of a peacock on the inside of her right forearm."

Tiffany had gotten the peacock tattoo with his brother when they had eloped in Vegas. The sergeant had their woman.

"She's the one we're looking for. Bring her into county lockup."

"No problem," the sergeant answered.

"And hey, thanks for tracking her down."

"Wasn't hard to find her. She was pulled over with a flat tire," the sergeant said. "Is it true that she's being investigated for her role in that homicide I heard about? The one in the mine?"

"News travels fast."

The sergeant laughed. "There are no secrets in our line of work, brother." The man hung up.

Blake shifted in her seat like she could hear their conversation. Jeremy reached out and put his hand on her thigh.

She looked down at his hand. He'd wanted to be able to touch her like this for so long that it almost seemed too good to be true—like the world was just waiting for the opportunity to strike them down.

Maybe fate's weapon of choice was going to be Tiffany. It was impossible to know what she would tell them, but if everything went right, she would give them the last pieces of the puzzle.

With the closure of their investigation, it would likely be the end of his time with Blake. Their stolen moments would be the only things left to remember her by when he went back to his life in Missoula. Yet with only memories to keep him, he couldn't help the feeling that he would go back to a life that would be incomplete.

WHEN THEY ARRIVED at the station, Sergeant McDonald led them to the multimedia area where the soft interrogation room was being broadcast across the monitors. The room on the screens had pictures of trees and birds, magazines were strewn across the coffee table and there was an overstuffed couch. The place had more in common with a doctor's waiting room than a regular interrogation room, which usually held nothing more than a table and a plastic chair that got hard on the perpetrator's behind after a few hours of sitting around and waiting.

"How long has she been in there?" Jeremy asked.

"About an hour. Maybe a little longer," the sergeant said. "She was a spitfire when she came in. Apparently this isn't how she wanted to spend her afternoon."

"Did you find out where she was going?"

The sergeant reached up and gripped the top of his bulletproof vest in his resting position. "I caught her at the northern edge of the county, heading toward Canada. There was a gas station map on the passenger's seat. I bet you money she was trying to figure out a back road that could get her out of the country—that was, until she got the flat. You're damn lucky we caught up to her."

They were lucky, but why had Tiffany been running? Only the guilty ran; the innocent stayed put.

"You got her from here?" Sergeant McDonald asked.

Jeremy nodded. "Thanks again."

The sergeant gave them a quick two-finger wave and left the room, looking happier than hell that this wasn't his problem anymore.

Jeremy gave a light laugh.

"Something funny?" Blake asked, crossing her good arm over her chest as she leaned against the wall.

"Nope," he said, pulling himself together. "You want to go in there with me?"

"I'm supposed to be on leave. If I go in there, our entire investigation will be compromised. Anything she says might not be admissible in court. We have to make sure to follow protocol."

He stepped closer to her and moved in to kiss her, but stopped as he remembered they were in the station. No one was around, but they still needed to keep it as private as they could.

Blake moved away, almost as if she was thinking the same thing—or was she thinking something else? Was it possible she regretted sleeping with him?

"You need to get in there," Blake said, motioning toward the interrogation room. "If Ms. Davy is involved, then it's only a matter of time before she runs. She has the money to go anywhere, anytime. If she gets loose, there's little to no chance that we'll get her back."

Blake was right, but he wasn't ready to let things go between them. He wanted answers. Leaving his heart open and exposed wasn't something he was used to.

He tipped his head as he forced himself to stay quiet about what was going on inside. Whether he wanted them to or not, his feelings could wait.

Jeremy turned to go out of the media room.

"Wait," Blake called after him. He turned back. "Good luck in there. I hope you get the answers you need."

"You mean the answers *we* need." He closed the door as he made his way out and across the hall. At the door to the interrogation room, he took a long breath and forced himself to focus on the task at hand. He pushed opened the door, seeing Tiffany seated in a corner of the sofa, her arms crossed over her chest like she was protecting herself from attack.

"Well, well, Tiffany," he said as he took a seat across the room. "Long time, no see."

In truth, he'd been in the woman's presence only a handful of times, and the last time he'd seen her had been a little over three years ago. She had changed. Her dark hair had more gray and her face was now so thin that her tan skin hung loose on her cheeks. She looked haggard. In a way, he found comfort in the fact she was stressed. It proved that she was feeling something about Robert's death. Whether it was guilt or sadness he had yet to find out.

Tiffany glared at him. "What in the hell are you doing here?"

"Thought I'd come for a visit. Catch up. A

lot's changed in the last few days with Robert's death and all."

Anger sparked in her eyes, and she opened her mouth to speak but held back.

He was getting a reaction. *Good.* Truth could be found in moments when emotions reigned.

"Did you really think you would get away with it?"

Her face contorted with rage. "I didn't shoot Robert."

"If you didn't do it, why haven't you come forward? You had to have known we were looking for you. Instead you ran. I'm sure you can understand why we have you sitting in cuffs right now."

"I didn't want to get caught up in all of Robert's crap. I'm so tired of it."

"Well, lucky for you, Robert's affairs are now yours."

Tiffany cringed. "I don't want nothing of his."

"Other than the money you took out of the bank last week, you mean?"

"I took the money because I was leaving his sorry behind. What does that have to do with anything?" Tiffany raised her chin in indignation.

"Nothing, but it sure is strange that you wipe out the bank accounts, then disappear just around the time your husband was murdered. Don't you think?"

"Look, I took the money, but I didn't kill your brother. We had our problems, but I never wanted him dead."

"Did you want to threaten my partner, Deputy West, and her family?"

"Deputy West? You mean Blake?"

"You on a first-name basis?"

Tiffany rolled her eyes, the movement almost

adolescent and in direct contrast to the wrinkles that surrounded her lips. "I've met her a few times."

"And?" He motioned for her to continue.

"She's been up to Robert's and my place, breaking up fights. I ain't got no problem with her. If anything, she's saved me from spending a few nights in jail over the years. I wouldn't want nothing bad to happen to her. Don't she have a kid?"

Jeremy nodded.

He wasn't positive, but from the way she spoke and the way her body seemed to relax, he guessed she was telling the truth. But just because she didn't have something to do with the threat on Blake didn't mean she didn't have a hand in Robert's murder.

"You guys like to fight? You and Robert?"

"You know how it has been between him and I. Nothing ever changed."

"So you killed him?"

"I told you, Jeremy, I didn't kill your stupid brother," she said, looking him square in the eye. "There were days where I hated his guts, but I ain't stupid."

"What do you mean by that, Tiffany?"

She snorted. "Everybody in this whole damn county knows about me and your brother. We had some good fights over the years." She paused and looked away. She gave a reminiscent chuckle. "It's what made us *us*, you know?"

One thing he knew well was couples fighting. His parents had done it for so long that he still had nightmares of some of their fights from his childhood. It must have been the same for Robert, but unlike him, Robert had chosen to perpetuate the unhealthy cycle their parents had taught them.

If things worked out with Blake, they couldn't be like the rest of his family. It would be hard, but he couldn't let their relationship fall down the path his brother had taken.

"Do you know if Todd bought a gun in the weeks before Robert's death?"

Tiffany's face darkened as she nodded. "He bought it off the mayor, and then he got the dang thing stolen. I kept telling him to shut up about that gun, but he never listened… But I'm telling you, I don't have nothing to do with what's going on."

He nodded. "Why did Todd O'Brien have your car?"

Her cheeks turned ruddy, and a thin sheen of sweat developed on her forehead as she bit her lip. She ran her hands down the legs of her pants, drying them.

"Tell me the truth, Tiffany. That's the only way you are going to get anywhere here."

"Todd and I are friends." The redness in her cheeks darkened.

"How *good* of friends?" He knew the answer, but he had to have her admission.

She looked away. "We been dating on and off for a while now. 'Bout six months maybe."

"Did Todd have something to do with Robert's death? Had Robert found out about you two?"

"Robert knew. I moved out of our house about a month ago. The last time Blake was up I said, 'Enough is enough,' and got the hell out of there. Todd ain't no peach, but he's better than that brother of yours. All Robert ever cared about was that stinking mine."

"Would you say you *hated* Robert?"

She didn't look at him. "If you knew your brother like I did, you woulda hated him, too."

In their adult lives, he and his brother hadn't been close, but he hadn't hated Robert. Yet it wasn't hard to imagine how Tiffany could have gotten there.

"Did you want to get back at him for the way he treated you by having Todd force him off his land?"

Her eyes flew to his. "How in the hell do you know that?"

It was as good as an admission. She'd been in on Robert's buyout. "What about the tax lien? Was that part of your or Todd's doing?"

"I didn't have nothing to do with that. That was all Todd's idea. If he wouldn't have been such an idiot, we could have found another way, but he was cash poor. Stupid man got mixed up in something he shoulda never been messing with."

"How's that?"

Tiffany rubbed her hands on her legs again, leaving behind a line of sweat. "He shoulda never got wrapped up with the mayor and his wife. Those two are nothing more than money-hungry vipers. I told him. And look where it got him—a one-room suite in the ICU."

Todd would be lucky if he ever left that hospital, but Jeremy said nothing.

"If you want to know who murdered my husband, look to them. Those two will stop at nothing to get what they want."

"What do you mean by that?"

"Those two have been using Todd as the front man to scoop up land around the Foreman Mine for years. If you look at the map,

Todd's name is on most of the land that makes up the ravine that the Foreman Mine sits on."

"Why do they have him buying up the land?"

Tiffany gave him an are-you-really-that-ignorant kind of look. "They have a lot of irons in the fire. Because of their company and the fact that John holds an office, it would blow back on them if they were ever caught buying up county foreclosures. So they set it up, and Todd signs his name on the dotted lines. He gets one hell of a kickback."

"Why do they want all this land?"

Tiffany sighed like he was a pain in her butt. "Robert's mine has been doing good. His claim sits right in the middle of a major source of copper ore. It could be worth millions, or more, depending on their buyer."

"What do you mean, depending on their

buyer? Aren't they trying to get a mine in there?"

Tiffany shook her head. "Their company is going through hard times. Tartarus Environmental Investments has been putting out money hand over fist to get the mineral rights to the area along the vein. Right now they couldn't afford to get a bulldozer, let alone the money it would take to put in a full-scale mine."

"So they're putting the land together to sell?"

Tiffany nodded. "And it hinges on Robert's claim. The Japanese buyers won't make a move until the parcel is complete and they have open mineral rights. Judith was desperate. She was afraid that if they didn't act quick, the buyers would walk. She couldn't wait for the tax lien to go to auction. Normally that would have worked, but Robert had started to look for a lawyer. He wanted to take them down. He was threatening them. Hell, he even threatened Todd."

"So Robert knew that your friends were all working together to take his land?"

Tiffany looked down at her hands, like all of a sudden she felt bad for her role in stripping his brother of his land, but it didn't lessen the fact that, in a way, she'd had a hand in Robert's death. Everyone who had been involved with the mayor and his wife had had a hand in his brother's murder, but the only one he could arrest was the one who had pulled the trigger.

"I didn't want things to go down like this. I hated Robert, but I never wanted him dead. It was all Judith's idea. They had to save their business. They couldn't risk a lawsuit or the political ramifications that would happen if their dealings came to light. If Robert had acted, the buyers would have certainly backed out of the deal."

He thought about the phone call they had overheard at Ms. Davy's house. No wonder she had been in a rush for them to leave. She'd been trying to save a deal years in the making…a deal that, if it had fallen through, would have ruined her and her husband's company.

It all made sense, but there was only one sure way to know if Tiffany was telling the truth about the mayor and his wife. "Can I see your hands?"

Tiffany frowned. "Why?"

He thought back to the fingerprint the techs had pulled from the murder weapon. The techs had determined the person who'd fired the gun that killed Robert had a scar on his or her index finger. Now he needed to see Tiffany's.

"Just let me see them."

Tiffany stuck out her hands. Her fingernails were short and had dirt stuck underneath. He turned her hands over. Her index fingers were unmarred. She wasn't their killer.

"Can you sign your name for me?" he asked, pulling a pen from his pocket and handing it to her.

She took the pen.

"Right there on the magazine is fine," he said, pointing toward *Good Housekeeping*.

She signed with her right hand. This meant she hadn't left the note at Blake's house, because whoever had written it was left-handed, according to Casper.

He didn't have the killer...but he had the one who would help him break the case.

"Thanks," he said, taking his pen back and slipping it in his pocket. "How well do you know Ms. Davy?"

Tiffany shrugged. "We used to be friends. Real good friends, up until lately. We never should have mixed business and friendship."

"Do you know if Judith has a scar?"

"A scar?"

"On her hand or fingers possibly?"

Tiffany sat back against the couch as she thought for a moment. "She's a smart woman, likes to get involved and to know how their money is being spent. A few years ago she was up at the mines. There was an accident with some of the explosives, nothing major, but she had to have stitches."

Jeremy's skin tingled as it always did when he was close to catching his suspect. Judith Davy knew explosives…and probably just the right amount to collapse the mouth of a mine.

"If what you're saying is true, then you are

going to need protective custody. Your life may be in danger."

"Why do you think I had to leave?" Tiffany scoffed. "You can't mess with people like the mayor and his wife and not expect to get hurt."

Jeremy had everything he needed. He had his probable cause. All they needed now was to take Judith Davy into custody and get her prints. Once they matched, they had their killer.

Chapter Twenty-One

The evening air had taken on a cold edge, the kind that promised snow was just over the horizon. Blake had always loved this time of year, the end of an era, the start of a world masked with white and waiting for the rebirth that would come in the spring. More than anything it promised a refreshing change.

The lights were on in the shop that sat just at the end of Judith Davy's driveway. As they neared she could make out a brand-new Mercedes and Mayor Engelman's Land Rover, complete with vanity plates that read *NMBR1*. She snickered. His reign as number one was about to be over. In a matter of minutes, he would be married to a woman cuffed and stuffed in the back of a squad car.

Hopefully if the district attorney dug deep into this case, they would be able to finish pulling the legal threads that would also put John Engelman in the hot seat, but knowing him, he probably had his lawyer on speed dial. Then again, even people like Engelman screwed up. If they didn't, she and Jeremy wouldn't have been rolling up their driveway with an arrest warrant.

Jeremy stepped out of the car carrying the warrant the judge had given him before she even had it in Park.

"Hey, wait up," she called after him. "We don't know how she's going to respond here, so you need to be careful."

He stopped and waited for her to catch up. "I doubt she's going to do anything stupid. She has her posse here. The only thing we need to worry about is doing things right."

"What do you mean?"

"Look," he said, pointing to the Mercedes. "Who drives a Mercedes AMG S65 in this state? That car right there costs more than two hundred thousand dollars brand-new."

She stared at the car. It was pretty, but who needed a car that cost more than some houses?

"That has to be their lawyer," Jeremy said. "No doubt the judge who signed off on the arrest warrant was the same man who gave the mayor and his wife a call to let them know we were on our way. The call to their lawyer was probably the first one they made as soon as they found out."

The made their way up to the house and its hand-carved door. They didn't have to knock.

The door swung open, and Mayor Engelman stood waiting, his arms crossed over his chest and an angry look on his face. "As soon as this is over, your asses won't be able to get a job at Dairy Queen."

Jeremy smiled at the threat. "It's okay, Mr. Mayor. I never liked ice cream anyway."

The mayor's cheeks reddened, and his lips tightened with rage. "You stupid son of a—"

"Stop." Judith Davy stepped to the mayor's side and put her hand on his arm. "Everything will be fine. Won't it, Mr. Deschamps?" She turned to the gray-haired man who walked beside her.

Mr. Deschamps made his way over to them and looked them up and down. "If the investigation is anything like these two Barney Fifes,

I think we'll have you out of jail and free and clear of all charges in a matter of days, Ms. Davy."

"Being charged with murder isn't quite like getting a speeding ticket," Blake said, unable to keep quiet any longer. "The press and the DA are going to have a field day with this. There's nothing the public likes better than the guilty—especially the indulgent overentitled snobs of the world—getting what they deserve."

"And what exactly is it that you think I deserve, little pig?" Ms. Davy sneered.

"Not only did you murder my friend's brother—you threatened my family." Blake stepped closer so she could look straight into the woman's eyes. "*No one* will ever get away with hurting the people I love. Not you. Not your husband."

"Oh, honey, did you hear that?" Ms. Davy

said with a patronizing smirk. "Isn't her little threat cute?"

"May I please see your hands, Ms. Davy?" Jeremy asked.

She looked to her lawyer, who gave an acknowledging tip of the head. She stuck out her hands. On the index finger of her left hand was a long, jagged scar.

"Would you please step outside, Ms. Davy, and put your hands on the wall?" Jeremy asked, but the tone in his voice made it clear it was an order.

She followed his orders. "Frisk away. This will be the one and only time you'll ever get to touch me."

Jeremy ran his hands over the woman's body, looking for hidden weapons, but she was clear. He slipped the cuffs on her.

As they made their way back to the car, Judith turned back to her husband and the lawyer. "I'll see you in a few days. There's bail money in the safe."

Mr. Engelman nodded, but he turned away from his wife like he knew that this was something they would fight, but it was one thing his wife would never walk away from.

This time, their greed had gone too far.

Chapter Twenty-Two

Things with the mayor would only get worse, but at least they had the person responsible for Robert's death behind bars. Even so, Blake's heart was heavy. Everything was over…including her time with Jeremy. The back door leading to his parents' patio opened and Jeremy walked out carrying two pints.

"Want a beer?" he asked, lifting one of the cups.

"Sure, thanks," she said, forcing a small smile as he handed it to her.

Her mother and Megan were out in the backyard with Jeremy's parents. They were all sitting around a fire pit, laughing and joking as they roasted marshmallows. She should have felt happy, surrounded by the people she cared about, but she couldn't let go of her uneasy sadness.

"I bet you're relieved. Sounds like Captain Prather's going to reinstate you once the investigation clears."

She nodded, thumbing the edge of the cold glass. "Yeah, but I'm still going to have to deal with the mayor."

"Until the next election."

"A lot can happen between now and then," she said, then took a long pull from the hops-flavored beer.

"He can't fire you. Not without the threat of a lawsuit anyway."

Jeremy was right, but it didn't make her feel

any better. The weight of politics and the re-percussions of this investigation would hang over her until the end of her career, at least if she continued working in Butte.

She turned to him as he sat down next to her. The late-evening sun caught the bits of red and amber in his hair and made him look even more handsome, but his eyes were filled with concern and a heaviness she hadn't seen in them before.

"Have you ever thought about leaving?" he asked, looking down at the beer in his hands.

She considered it for a moment. "If I left, everything would change, Jeremy. We'd have to move. Start over. Megan would have to change schools. My mother would never want to leave her home. She's lived here forever." She looked over at her mother and her daughter.

She was struck by how much her daughter

looked like her. The same unruly blond hair, the same blue eyes, even the way she looked around at the world, like she was just waiting for the next thing to happen. Would she grow up and make the same mistakes?

Blake shook her head at the thought. Something had to change. Somehow she needed to save her daughter from this world of fires and death while at the same time teach her how strong they could be. Perhaps she could even show her that there were good men out there, men who had hearts of gold and could look past the imperfections in a person and just love them for who and what they were.

She could teach her how to live a healthy life, one centered on family, hope and trust.

"I talked to the captain in Missoula today." Jeremy took a draw from his beer.

She tensed. "When do you have to go back to work?"

"In a couple of days. But that's not why I called him." Jeremy reached over and took her hand. "He said that there is a job there for you in the city if you want it. It would be a little different, definitely busier than the sheriff's department, but the pay would be higher. I could help you get your mother set up, and there are fantastic schools for Megan. She'd have her choice. She could even go to the same school as Penny if she wanted to."

Blake's body tingled with excitement. Was this something she really wanted? She looked at Jeremy, searching his eyes. He had to love her if he was helping her to build a new future. Didn't he?

"If you don't want to move, I can come to Butte. My parents' lawyer has read Robert's will. According to the terms, Tiffany gets nothing. Everything goes to my parents."

"Tiffany gets nothing?"

Jeremy shook his head. "I think that may have been part of the reason she had wanted him to lose everything…why she had been behind Todd's buyout."

"Can your parents afford to pay off the tax lien?"

Jeremy shrugged. "I think so, but if you wanted, we could pay it. We could become miners…if you wanted to stay in Butte. I would do whatever it takes to make you happy."

It was noble that Jeremy was taking steps to stop Tartarus Environmental Investments from getting their hands on his brother's land, but he had told her he never wanted to mine. He was willing to compromise who he was for her, but she didn't want him to. Not like this.

"We can't stay here, Jeremy."

"Are you saying you want to move to Missoula with me?"

She couldn't help the feeling of love that filled her, but was love enough of a reason to leave her home? To build a new life? Falling in love was a risk…

But there was nothing that she wanted more than to follow her heart.

"I…I think I'll take the job." Her body tensed. "And, if it's okay, I want my mom to go with us. She drives me crazy sometimes, but she's my best friend. I don't know what I'd do without her."

"I thought you might say that. If you want, we can look for a house—one with plenty of space." Jeremy smiled as he set down his glass. "But first, I have something for you."

He reached in his pocket. "I know this is fast, and I have no idea what you are going to say, but I've been thinking… I want to do this right. I've loved you since we were kids. I know things haven't always gone as we've wanted them to, but I love you and I always will." He got down on his knee in front of her. "The other night, after the fire, I went back and took a branch of the tree. It took me a few hours, but I carved this for you." He opened his hand. In his palm was a ring made of wood.

Her heartbeat thundered in her ears, making it almost impossible to hear him as he spoke.

"You told me that you always thought of that tree as a metaphor for you and your life. I don't know if you meant it as a good thing or a bad thing, or both, but as I thought about it, all I could think about was how beautiful it was. A tree lives its entire life supporting the lives around it, the grass at its feet and the leaves on its branches. You are just like the tree, loving and supporting those around you. I love that about you. And when you look at this ring, I want you to see that even when we get burnt by life, you can always have a new beginning."

He took her trembling hand and slipped it on her ring finger. It fit perfectly. "If you want, this ring can be a symbol of our promise to create a new future…a life with each other."

"I…I…" she whispered, moving her hand right and left as she looked at the ring's swirling pattern.

He reached up and cupped her face. "I love you."

Tears filled her eyes, but she tried to blink them back. "I love you, too." She got down on her knees and buried her face into his neck. She let her tears fall.

For once it felt good to be measured by time. Their love wouldn't last seconds or minutes or hours. No. Their love would last a lifetime.

* * * * *